Anthony Gilbert and The Murder Room

》》 This title is part of The Murder Room, our series dedicated to making available out-of-print or hard-to-find titles by classic crime writers.

Crime fiction has always held up a mirror to society. The Victorians were fascinated by sensational murder and the emerging science of detection; now we are obsessed with the forensic detail of violent death. And no other genre has so captivated and enthralled readers.

Vast troves of classic crime writing have for a long time been unavailable to all but the most dedicated frequenters of second-hand bookshops. The advent of digital publishing means that we are now able to bring you the backlists of a huge range of titles by classic and contemporary crime writers, some of which have been out of print for decades.

From the genteel amateur private eyes of the Golden Age and the femmes fatales of pulp fiction, to the morally ambiguous hard-boiled detectives of mid twentieth-century America and their descendants who walk our twenty-first century streets, The Murder Room has it all. 》》

The Murder Room
Where Criminal Minds Meet

themurderroom.com

T0352511

Anthony Gilbert (1899–1973)

Anthony Gilbert was the pen name of Lucy Beatrice Malleson. Born in London, she spent all her life there, and her affection for the city is clear from the strong sense of character and place in evidence in her work. She published 69 crime novels, 51 of which featured her best known character, Arthur Crook, a vulgar London lawyer totally (and deliberately) unlike the aristocratic detectives, such as Lord Peter Wimsey, who dominated the mystery field at the time. She also wrote more than 25 radio plays, which were broadcast in Great Britain and overseas. Her thriller *The Woman in Red* (1941) was broadcast in the United States by CBS and made into a film in 1945 under the title *My Name is Julia Ross*. She was an early member of the British Detection Club, which, along with Dorothy L. Sayers, she prevented from disintegrating during World War II. Malleson published her autobiography, *Three-a-Penny*, in 1940, and wrote numerous short stories, which were published in several anthologies and in such periodicals as *Ellery Queen's Mystery Magazine* and *The Saint*. The short story 'You Can't Hang Twice' received a Queens award in 1946. She never married, and evidence of her feminism is elegantly expressed in much of her work.

By Anthony Gilbert

Scott Egerton series

Tragedy at Freyne (1927)

The Murder of Mrs
  Davenport (1928)

Death at Four Corners (1929)

The Mystery of the Open
  Window (1929)

The Night of the Fog (1930)

The Body on the Beam (1932)

The Long Shadow (1932)

The Musical Comedy
  Crime (1933)

An Old Lady Dies (1934)

The Man Who Was Too
  Clever (1935)

**Mr Crook Murder
  Mystery series**

Murder by Experts (1936)

The Man Who Wasn't
  There (1937)

Murder Has No Tongue (1937)

Treason in My Breast (1938)

The Bell of Death (1939)

Dear Dead Woman (1940)

 aka *Death Takes a Redhead*

The Vanishing Corpse (1941)

 aka *She Vanished in the Dawn*

The Woman in Red (1941)

 aka *The Mystery of the
 Woman in Red*

Death in the Blackout (1942)

 aka *The Case of the Tea-
 Cosy's Aunt*

Something Nasty in the
  Woodshed (1942)

 aka *Mystery in the Woodshed*

The Mouse Who Wouldn't
  Play Ball (1943)

 aka *30 Days to Live*

He Came by Night (1944)

 aka *Death at the Door*

The Scarlet Button (1944)

 aka *Murder Is Cheap*

A Spy for Mr Crook (1944)

The Black Stage (1945)

 aka *Murder Cheats the Bride*

Don't Open the Door (1945)

 aka *Death Lifts the Latch*

Lift Up the Lid (1945)

 aka *The Innocent Bottle*

The Spinster's Secret (1946)

 aka *By Hook or by Crook*

Death in the Wrong Room
  (1947)

Die in the Dark (1947)

 aka *The Missing Widow*

Death Knocks Three Times
  (1949)

Murder Comes Home (1950)

A Nice Cup of Tea (1950)

 aka *The Wrong Body*

Lady-Killer (1951)

Miss Pinnegar Disappears (1952)
aka *A Case for Mr Crook*

Footsteps Behind Me (1953)
aka *Black Death*

Snake in the Grass (1954)
aka *Death Won't Wait*

Is She Dead Too? (1955)
aka *A Question of Murder*

And Death Came Too (1956)

Riddle of a Lady (1956)

Give Death a Name (1957)

Death Against the Clock (1958)

Death Takes a Wife (1959)
aka *Death Casts a Long Shadow*

Third Crime Lucky (1959)
aka *Prelude to Murder*

Out for the Kill (1960)

She Shall Die (1961)
aka *After the Verdict*

Uncertain Death (1961)

No Dust in the Attic (1962)

Ring for a Noose (1963)

The Fingerprint (1964)

The Voice (1964)
aka *Knock, Knock! Who's There?*

Passenger to Nowhere (1965)

The Looking Glass Murder (1966)

The Visitor (1967)

Night Encounter (1968)
aka *Murder Anonymous*

Missing from Her Home (1969)

Death Wears a Mask (1970)
aka *Mr Crook Lifts the Mask*

Murder is a Waiting Game (1972)

Tenant for the Tomb (1971)

A Nice Little Killing (1974)

Standalone Novels

The Case Against Andrew Fane (1931)

Death in Fancy Dress (1933)

The Man in Button Boots (1934)

Courtier to Death (1936)
aka *The Dover Train Mystery*

The Clock in the Hatbox (1939)

The Clock in the Hatbox

Anthony Gilbert

An Orion book

Copyright © Lucy Beatrice Malleson 1939

The right of Lucy Beatrice Malleson to be identified as the author of this work has been asserted in accordance with the Copyright, Designs and Patents Act 1988.

This edition published by
The Orion Publishing Group Ltd
Orion House
5 Upper St Martin's Lane
London WC2H 9EA

An Hachette UK company
A CIP catalogue record for this book is available from the British Library

ISBN 978 1 4719 1066 1

www.orionbooks.co.uk

ONE

THE judge was finishing his summing up.

> *"The verdict, therefore, gentlemen of the jury,
> would appear to turn on the question—who put the
> clock in the hat box? If, beyond all shadow of
> doubt, you are convinced that that hand belonged
> to the prisoner, then you have no option but to
> bring in a verdict of guilty. But if you believe that
> there exists the smallest doubt on this point, I am
> bound to remind you that under English law a pris-
> oner must be found guilty of the crime of which he
> is accused to the complete satisfaction of you all,
> without the smallest question; unless, therefore, you
> are all so satisfied, you must find her innocent of
> this murder."*

He added his usual warning, told us that if we wanted
any further help in coming to a decision he would be
at our disposal, and we uncurled ourselves and filed out.

It had been a long case and a painful one. The
woman in the dock was known to us all. She had been
living among us ever since her marriage to the dead
man eleven years earlier. In a community like ours no
one's life belongs entirely to himself. We knew a good
deal about one another's affairs and we speculated a lot

more. Viola Ross was the kind of person who invites gossip. She had married, at twenty-three, a man twice her age, a widower with a son at school. When Ross brought her back with him, after a visit he had been paying to a sick sister, we all gasped. It's one of the mysteries of life how men of his type contrive to attract and marry women of hers. He was a pepper-and-salt little man, a bit thin on top even then, with fair hair that straggled above a high bony forehead, a habit of making a suit look five years old and shapeless when he had worn it twice, and an absent manner that made him the butt—not always in a very friendly way—of most of his colleagues. She, on the other hand, was the Rossetti type, a deep-bosomed auburn-haired woman. You turned to look after her if you met her on the street, and you went on remembering her long after she was out of sight. I admit I was a good deal moved by the sight of her in the dock. There was something so desperately alive about her, so real and solid. I thought sometimes what a magnificent courtesan she'd have made if she had been born of another race and time.

Of course, in a town as small as Marston, she was bound to attract attention and provoke gossip. I remember Ross's thin freckled face positively shivering with pride when he brought her back from their three-day honeymoon; I had happened to be passing when he got out of the car and stood on the pavement to give her a hand. She had looked around as if accepting my homage, the homage of any man for that matter, as a natural corollary.

She wasn't, I think, as popular with the women from

2

the very start as she was with the men; that kind of woman seldom is. They used to look at her a bit askance and hang rather obviously on their husbands' arms when she was by. But the men would have done anything for her.

The extraordinary thing is that none of us knew what she did with herself all day. She didn't seem to have any special activities. She didn't play bridge—but then, neither did Teddy, and he didn't encourage her in any amusement that might take her away from the house when he was in it. She didn't golf or play tennis, she couldn't even drive a car, but she never gave you the impression of being an idle woman or a bored one. She seemed content just to be. Music was her great resource, and we supposed she put into that all the dissatisfactions she must have experienced as Teddy Ross's wife. For it was an empty kind of life. They had no children; the boy, Harry, only came for the holidays and often not then; Teddy boasted that he had only been to the movies once in his life and hadn't thought much of it, didn't dance—though she was a beautiful dancer, given the chance—in short, he resembled one of those small animals that live in a burrow and feel it's a great adventure every time they get a glimpse of the light.

Teddy, at the time of his marriage and also at the time of his death, was mathematics master at St. Hilary's, the rather famous local school. His hobbies were chess and crosswords, and a primer on his own subject that he died without completing. For a time after their marriage he wore Viola with the same self-conscious boastfulness and pride that he might have felt toward an orchid in his buttonhole. But after a bit I suppose he got used to her.

Harry Ross must have been nine or ten when his father married Viola, and he and his stepmother didn't meet much until he was about eighteen and going to college. I suppose he took after his mother—there was nothing of Teddy about him—a tall dark fellow, with glossy hair and shining eyes and a great fund of vitality. I soon saw that Viola had the same effect on him that she had on most men. He didn't feel absolutely at home with her, but she fascinated him.

There was one other member of the household at the time of Teddy's death—his secretary, Irene Cobb—a plain, efficient, worthy young woman of about thirty. I suppose you could hardly have found a greater contrast than Irene and Viola; she was earnest, thought everything Teddy did admirable, and was honored because she was sometimes allowed to work overtime without pay on the precious text book that occupied most of Teddy's spare time.

Irene tried to adopt a sisterly attitude toward young Harry. I know she once called him "Old Man," because he told me about it.

"Your father's going to be tremendously proud of you, I know, old man," she said.

"Trying to suggest she's part of the harem," said Harry disgustedly. I rather agreed with him. Miss Cobb had one or two tremendous female friendships, and she belonged to the local amateur dramatic society. In fact, that was where I met her. She had no gift for acting and loudly proclaimed her knowledge of the fact, but this never deterred her from accepting a part or offering to understudy or stage-manage.

Now I come to think about it, it is amazing how quiet Viola Ross seemed to be. For all that vitality and color of hers, she could sink into her surroundings as a partridge sinks into the ground and be practically invisible. Of course, Teddy was always in to meals and all her persuasions could scarcely coax him out in the evenings, but all the same she had a good deal of time on her hands.

People used to speculate about her private life. It was incredible that Teddy should satisfy her, particularly as, about five years after the marriage, he developed a weak heart and moved into a room of his own. Viola used to go up to London to attend concerts, and the uncharitable found something peculiar in that. But no one could bring any charge against her of neglecting her husband.

The first hint of trouble was when Harry came back last summer. He was nearing his twenty-first birthday, as striking in his own way as Viola in hers. He woke that house up. He chafed at his father's restrictions, at his early hours, his lack of visitors, at his pet economies, and the general dullness of the scheme of things. Also he told Teddy that he didn't want to be a schoolmaster, he'd rather go abroad, live what he called a man's life. Teddy told him, not without reason, that he might have thought of that before going to college, where he had contrived to spend an unconscionable amount of money.

"I didn't know how much I'd loathe it," said Harry.

"It's taken you three years to find out."

"I thought I might as well stay up and get my degree."

I can imagine Teddy's snort at that. "Your degree indeed!"

"It's called the Gentleman's Tripos." There was nothing of the velvet glove about Harry.

Teddy was annoyed and showed it; the whole town knew that there was trouble brewing, and I fancy Harry didn't find the position improved when Viola suddenly came in violently on his side.

"You can't force him into a life he hates," she protested. "You might better cut his throat."

"You're ridiculous." I can imagine how Teddy would fume over that. "It's a good honorable career. . . ."

"He's only got one life." Viola would fling those words at him, head up, eyes vivid.

"Are you supporting my son against myself?"

"I want to make sure that a great injustice and a great wrong aren't done."

"You talk of my wronging Harry. . . ."

"Because you have the power, you can't force him to do something he hates. It's terrible—I mean, it's so fatally easy to make the wrong decision, and once it's made you have to abide by it forever."

I don't think for one moment that Teddy realized the implications of that. It is because of the armies of insensitive husbands that marriage has kept going as long as it has. A more observant man would have realized long ago that Viola regretted her marriage—but not Teddy. One effect, however, the conversation did have on him. He began to be suspicious of Viola's championship of the boy. It seemed to him incredible that a woman should side with a young man who wasn't even her own son against her husband. Ours being, as I have said, a place where gossip circulates freely, we presently heard that Teddy had decided to move back to his wife's room.

The breach between father and son widened. Young Harry went to London just before his twenty-first birthday; we heard that he was trying to make a living at journalism. He had a few pounds a year from his mother and now and again he sold something, so he struggled along somehow, but it must have been a bit of a change from his former comparative luxury—for whatever Teddy had done, he hadn't stinted the boy.

About this time, too, he began to be suspicious of Viola. He scrutinized her letters, examined her in detail as to her movements, even tried to listen in to her telephone calls. He said they didn't need a large staff, and cut the servants down to a sour-faced old maid called Martha, who acted as housekeeper, and a girl who came in by the day, going about nine o'clock in the evening. In short, he became the complete domestic tyrant, such as only little men of his stamp can become. It was when the situation was at its height, and was becoming increasingly acute, that Teddy suddenly died.

TWO

I TRIED to tell from the expressions on the faces of my fellow jurors their reactions to the evidence. I felt myself that, no matter what she had done, it would be infamous to stamp such a woman out of existence. She was so gorgeously vital, so radiant, so life-giving; even after her period of imprisonment, the tremendous ordeal she had undergone—for prosecuting counsel had spared her no conceivable humiliation—the fountain of her strength was not sapped. After three days, during which half the crimes of the calendar had been directly or by implication imputed to her, she remained quiet, unshaken, assured. I felt that, even if she had to hear the death sentence, she would remain unmoved.

Several of my neighbors were looking harassed for, I supposed, a variety of reasons. The responsibility of condemning a fellow creature to death is one from which the bravest may well shrink; others were genuinely perplexed by the evidence; and there were some whose thoughts I could see as clearly as though they were goldfish swimming and darting in a bowl. They were thinking that not so long ago Ross had been a fellow very like themselves, doing the day's work, listening to the radio at night, grumbling about the gas bills and the income tax, living with his wife in a house very similar to those in which they were themselves living —and now he was just mouldering bones and it looked uncommonly probable from the evidence that Mrs. Teddy was responsible. It made them shake a bit in their shoes, these complacent married men, accustomed to lording it over their wives and families. It made them realize that the most strong-minded husband isn't God Almighty and death can lurk in the most innocent guise. I reflected wryly that even guilty wives accomplish something for the community, something the very women who condemn them profit by, though they'd be horrified to admit it.

Morrison, our foreman, one of these big men to whom the weather isn't kind, dropped into a chair and mopped his forehead.

"Phew!" he said. "What a case! I should think they would exempt us from jury service for the next five years."

"Do you think she did it?" chirped a little gray man, looking like an antiquated bird. We all knew him; he kept the best bookshop in the place and was always recommending his customers to buy my novels.

"Good Lord, man, you don't expect me to tell you right off, do you? We've got to weigh the evidence, sift the grain from the chaff"—Morrison liked a Biblical tang to his conversation—"and then we shall all have to give our individual opinions, remembering that a woman's life is at stake."

"Rotten business, hanging women," muttered Chalmers.

A woman juror broke in in acid tones, "I hope some of you are going to spare a thought for the murdered man. Whatever happens to this woman she has brought on herself, but he was absolutely innocent."

Someone else said unexpectedly, "Well, it isn't much of a recommendation to any man to make his home life so unendurable that his wife is driven to murder —assuming she is guilty."

That started us on another line of argument that Morrison brought to an end by standing up again and saying, "Look here, this isn't getting us anywhere. We aren't here to discuss whether she had lovers or whether she didn't. It may be very reprehensible of her if she did, but it isn't a punishable offense. We're here to decide whether she did or did not smother Edward Ross on the night of April fourth."

"Has the prosecution established the fact that Mrs. Ross had a lover or lovers?" I inquired. "It seems to me that it has signally failed to do so. She herself has denied the suggestion and no evidence has been brought forward in support of the idea. The fact that she often went up to town alone means nothing."

"We know that Mr. Ross was very suspicious."

"God help women if that fact is going to be held as evidence against them."

Then Morrison called us to order again. "We must consider this case on the evidence and leave conjecture out of it," he warned. "We've got a good deal to go on, even so."

The affair had been very widely reported in the press; women of Mrs. Ross's class are not very frequently indicted for murder, and the woman's temperament and the circumstances of the affair had attracted general interest. Counsel for the Crown, a man called Hawkes, who had not belied his name, had dragged to light every incident and detail that by proof or implication could be used against her.

"Mrs. Ross, will you tell the court where you first met your husband?"

"When I was employed as a companion nurse to his sister, Mrs. White."

"How long had you been in her employ?"

"About ten months."

"I believe at that time you were under notice to go?"

"Yes."

"Will you tell the court why?"

Here Viola Ross's counsel lodged a protest, but the judge allowed the question.

"Mrs. White said she was making other arrangements."

"She gave you no other reason?"

"That was what she said."

"Isn't it the case that there had been trouble about your behavior with Mr. White?"

McNeile objected again, and this time the judge sided with him.

Hawkes put the question in another form. "If Mrs. White had not given you notice, would you have been prepared to stay?"

"Until something better turned up."

"So you were not going of your own free will?"

"No."

"And you had nothing in prospect?"

"At the time Mr. Ross came to stay Mrs. White had only just given me notice."

"You had nowhere to go, if you did not succeed in finding fresh employment when your notice had expired? No family or friends?"

"I should have found other work."

"Kindly answer the question."

"I had no family. My parents died when I was a child."

"You had no other relations?"

"None to whom I could have turned."

"None at all?"

"Only an aunt."

"And you couldn't have gone to her, even in an emergency?"

"No."

"Does that mean that you had quarreled with her?"

"We were not on good terms."

"Isn't it true that she had told you never to come near her house again?"

"I wouldn't have gone in any case."

Hawkes had the wisdom to let it go at that. He had created the impression for which he had been striving, an impression by no means favorable to the prisoner.

"So you had no alternative at the time that you met Mr. Ross? You had, I understand, very little money?"

"I had no money."

"And Mr. Ross proposed marriage almost at once?"

"At the end of a week."

"And you accepted him immediately?"

"I asked for twenty-four hours to think it over."

"And at the end of that time you accepted him?"

"Yes."

Hawkes leaned forward. "Why, Mrs. Ross? He was twice your age; he was scarcely the type of man to appeal to a young woman. He lived a very quiet life; you were young and spirited. Or are you asking the court to believe that you fell in love with this unassuming middle-aged man whom you had known only a few days?"

"I married him because I wished to, and because he wished it."

"Because he was your one alternative to starvation?"

"Not my only alternative."

"But your most pleasant alternative?"

"You might put it that way."

"I see." Hawkes flung back his head and jutted his prominent underlip. "Now, Mrs. Ross, I want you to answer one or two questions about your married life. You have been married for eleven years. Would you describe your marriage as a happy one?"

"I should describe it as an average marriage."

Hawkes turned an eloquent face to the jury. "You ask the court to believe that your marriage was typical?"

"For most of the time."

"Oh! Most of the time? Now, Mrs. Ross, I take it that your relations with your husband were those of any normal married couple?"

"At the time of his death—yes."

"But they had not always been?"

"For the first five years they were; then he had an illness that affected his heart, and on the suggestion of his doctor he moved into a room of his own. Recently, however, we had resumed relations."

"That would seem to imply that his health had improved?"

"He didn't ask the doctor's opinion in this case."

"But he must himself have felt that he was better."

"He may have done so."

"You can't answer me more certainly than that?"

"He didn't discuss the position with me. He simply told me what he wished."

"And you agreed?"

"Yes."

She hesitated before she answered that. I fancy I wasn't the only man on the jury who felt uncomfortable. Hawkes repeated his question.

"It seemed to me a little strange after so long, but since he was resolved—yes, I did agree."

"And your relations with your husband were quite friendly up to the time of his death?"

"I don't think I should say that. He hadn't forgiven me for siding with his son."

"I believe he had made a stipulation that you should not see Harry Ross?"

"Yes."

"A stipulation that you honored?"

"Not entirely."

"No? You mean, you did see him?"

"From time to time."

"In spite of your husband's prohibition?"

"I couldn't permit myself to be entirely ruled by him. The boy was very young and he had very little money."

"Am I to understand that you supplied him with money?"

"Once or twice."

"I think you told the court that you had no money of your own?"

"That is correct."

"So that the money you gave Harry Ross was actually his father's?"

"Harry was his son."

"A man is not bound to support his son when he comes of age, if he is acting directly contrary to his father's wishes."

"I don't believe that money should be allowed to ruin a young man's life."

"Ruin is a very strong word, Mrs. Ross."

"For a very tragic thing."

"You mean to imply that Harry Ross's life was in a fair way to be ruined?"

"If he couldn't get some money. It was a very small amount that I could send him."

"You didn't think it disloyal to your husband?"

"I suppose as a wife I had earned a little of my own to spend."

"And you chose to give that little to Harry Ross?"

"I've told you why."

"Have you, Mrs. Ross? You mean, because he was young and at the beginning of his career. A good many of us think that a young man should be independent."

"He hadn't been brought up to believe that he would suddenly find himself without money. His father had always made him a good allowance."

"You admit then that his father had treated him quite well?"

"So long as he fell in with his wishes."

"You believed you were right in helping to turn him from the plan originally made for him?"

"If I hadn't, I shouldn't have helped him."

"I see. Now, Mrs. Ross, I believe your husband found out that you were helping your stepson?"

"Yes."

"How was that?"

"Harry wrote to me for money."

"He wrote to you?"

"I had told him if he wanted money he had better write to me."

"He had no objection to taking money from you?"

"I told him that I could intercede with his father better than he could."

"And he believed you?"

"Why shouldn't he?"

"That isn't an answer to my question, Mrs. Ross."

The judge had leaned forward there and asked her if she would like to rest for a few minutes. She had been a long time in the witness box; McNeile had taken her story carefully and without haste, and now Hawkes was grilling her for all he was worth, which in legal circles was a good deal. The judge wanted to give her a chance to rest and pull herself together, but she thanked him and said she was quite ready to go on. I thought she was wise; she was gaining sympathy from the jury, who didn't care for Hawkes much more than I did. Now she replied to Hawkes' last question.

"He believed me, of course."

"Actually, however, you were not asking your husband for the money?"

"It would have been of no use."

"You did not let your stepson know that?"

"He wouldn't have taken the money, and I didn't want him to starve."

"Besides sending him the money you were also seeing him?"

"I went two or three times to his rooms."

"Your husband did not know that?"

"Not at first."

"When did he find out?"

"After he opened Harry's letter to me."

"Ah, he opened it?"

"Yes."

"Was he in the habit of opening your letters?"

"No. But I suppose he recognized the handwriting."

"He objected to his son writing to you?"

"He adopted the attitude that he had no son any longer."

"And this was because his son refused to follow in his own footsteps?"

"Yes."

"And that was his only reason?"

"So far as I know."

"You are sure, Mrs. Ross?"

"It's impossible ever to be sure of anything in another person's mind, but so far as I know that was the only reason."

Hawkes let that go. "After he had opened the letter, what happened?"

"He asked me if I had been helping Harry, and when I said that I had he was very angry."

"Did he say you were to discontinue that help at once?"

"Yes."

"And after that, did you help him?"

"Once more."

"Did you see him again?"

"I had to go up to London, so I took him the money in person. I wanted to warn him of the position."

"You could have written."

"I felt that letters were unsafe. Either my husband might contrive to get hold of it before it was mailed, or he might try to arrange to have it stopped."

"Suppose he had? Would there be anything in the letter that you would be afraid for him to know?"

"Naturally, I don't care to have my personal letters intercepted."

"Mrs. Ross, I must ask you to answer my questions You are pursuing a policy of systematic evasions. Believe me, these will do you no good with the jury. I ask you again, if you had written, would there have been anything in that letter that you wished your husband not to know?"

"When I saw my stepson I told him that I was finding the position intolerable, and that I was going to leave my husband."

"Had you told your husband that?"

"No. I intended to do so, but as it happened, he died very suddenly, as the court is aware."

"I understand. Now I put it to you, Mrs. Ross, that your husband was deeply suspicious of you?"

"In what way?"

"In every way."

She shrugged her fine shoulders. "That's very vague."

"It's a fact, isn't it, that he tried to read your correspondence?"

"He did."

"And to check up on your movements?"

"I wasn't aware of that until later."

"How much later?"

"At the inquest, when I heard my own servant confess that she had had instructions to keep a note of my visitors, my telephone calls, the letters I wrote or received."

"And up till that time you had not been aware how seriously he regarded the position?"

"He had always been inclined to be jealous."

"Of whom, Mrs. Ross?"

"Of anyone who was my friend, of my correspondents generally, of any excursion I took without him."

"I take it he had objected to your frequent visits to London?"

"When he could not accompany me—yes."

"And it was unusual for him to be able to accompany you?"

"He had his work."

"But you continued to make these journeys, in spite of his objections?"

"I have a great passion for music; it is impossible to hear good music in a place like Marston. I attended concerts in London, and I did not propose to rob myself of that pleasure."

"I think the jury understand. Now, Mrs. Ross, did your husband ever object to any particular company that you kept?"

"He had no grounds. He had placed a veto on my seeing my stepson, but that was all."

"He did not suggest that you went to London for any purpose except the reason that you gave him?"

"I've told you—he was suspicious of everything I did."

"Did you know that he was so suspicious that he had arranged for you to be shadowed on your visits to town?"

"I did not know, until the letter arrived the morning that we found him dead."

"That letter was from a firm of private detectives in London?"

"Yes."

"Asking them to make arrangements to trace your movements when you were in town, he having undertaken to supply them with the requisite information?"

"Yes. But I know no more of that than I could understand from the letter."

"Now, Mrs. Ross, do you wish the jury to understand that your husband never made any accusation to your face concerning any particular person whom you might come to London to meet?"

"Never."

"Remember you are speaking on oath."

"I have not forgotten it."

"I see. Now we will come to the night of your husband's death. You have told the court that on that evening he went upstairs to lie down for a couple of hours because he had a headache?"

"Yes."

"I think you said that you were occupying a double room at the time?"

"Yes, but as he was only lying down for a short time and intended to come downstairs and correct a stack of themes later on, he slept in his own room, which was across the landing. Then, if I wished to come to bed early, I should not disturb him."

"Was it customary for him to undress when he was only proposing to lie down for a couple of hours?"

"If he wished to sleep—yes."

"He was arranging to come down and work later?"

"At midnight."

"And you say that he had an alarm clock to wake him at that hour?"

"Yes. He always wound and set it himself."

"And he wound and set it that night?"

"I suppose so. I didn't see him."

"The witness, Miss Cobb, says that he did actually wind it."

"I don't doubt Miss Cobb's statement: I only say I didn't myself see it done."

"You never wound the clock?"

"No. I didn't even know how it worked. It was a new kind of which my husband was very proud."

"You say you couldn't have set it even if he had passed it to you?"

"No. I could have wound it, of course, but I knew nothing of the alarm part of it."

"I see. You are aware, of course, that the clock was subsequently found in a hat box in your husband's room?"

"Yes."

"Found by the police?"

"Yes."

"Didn't it surprise you that it should be in such an extraordinary place?"

"I could think of no conceivable explanation."

"If the police had not been called in, what would have happened to the clock?"

"I suppose it would have stayed in the hat box until I found it, going through my husband's effects."

"You had never known the clock placed in a hat box before?"

"Never. I shouldn't have noticed its absence myself. It was Miss Cobb who spoke of it."

"She asked where it was?"

"Yes. She used to work for my husband in his leisure time. She came around on the morning of the fifth and was horrified to hear that he was dead. She had been working with him until late the previous evening. She said he seemed tired and overworked, and had agreed when he said he thought it would be best for him to get a little sleep, and then come down, refreshed, to tackle his task. He went upstairs just before nine, and she went home at about the same time."

"And you?"

"I was restless, and as my husband was lying down and I did not expect to see him before morning I decided to go to a movie. That would be about nine-fifteen."

"Your husband did not know you had gone?"

"No. I expected to be back long before his alarm went off."

"You weren't going to tell him?"

"If he had asked me I would have told him. But I didn't go upstairs and deliberately interrupt him when he was trying to sleep."

"I see. Well, you went to the movies. Who was left in the house?"

"My husband and our housekeeper, Martha."

"So that if he wanted anything she would be able to attend to him?"

"I don't think she would do much. She always went to bed at ten, and she was as deaf as a post and could sleep through anything. It was very improbable, how-ever, that he would want anything. She would leave whiskey and soda in the library in case my husband required any, but he was a very abstemious man and scarcely ever touched anything."

"Yes. So you went out. And you came back soon after eleven?"

"Yes. I let myself in with my latch key, glanced into

the library, that was in darkness, and went up to bed."

"And you knew nothing of your husband's death until the next morning?"

"Martha came in and told me that she was afraid there was something wrong. I went into my husband's room—I thought he had had a heart attack. I rang up the doctor, and when he came he told me he thought it was his heart. He seemed quite satisfied with the position, and said he would send me a death certificate."

"When did you begin to suspect?"

"I suspected nothing until the matter of the alarm clock came up. That was due to Miss Cobb. She arrived at nine o'clock with some papers she had typed overnight; she used to work for a local firm during the day, and in the evenings she worked for my husband. The girl who opened the door told her what had happened, and immediately she became hysterical. She insisted on forcing her way into the house, and actually went into the room where my husband's body was before she could be prevented."

"And it was she who noticed the absence of the clock?"

"Yes. She looked around the room, I am told, and asked what had happened. Then suddenly she cried, 'Where's the clock?' Naturally, I did not know. I could only suppose that the clock had not been set after all."

"Did you see Miss Cobb?"

"Yes, as soon as I realized that she was in the house. I had to beg her to go; she created quite a scene."

"Is it true that she said, 'You'll be glad now. You've been waiting for this'?"

"I really couldn't tell you what was said. She was quite beside herself."

"Still, she did make definite accusations?"

"She was quite unbalanced. She talked at the top of her voice for some minutes before I could quiet her. I have no doubt my servants could recall what she said better than I."

"What happened about the clock?"

"I assured her that I had not seen it, had known nothing of it. She looked wildly around and said, 'Clocks don't walk off on their own legs; and he had it last night. Where is it now?' I said that probably my husband had taken it downstairs when he went to correct his themes, and that it would be found in the library. However, when we came to examine the books we found they had not been touched, and from various details it seemed obvious that my husband had never left the room."

"Did you pay much attention to Miss Cobb?"

"Candidly, very little. Nor did I think a second time about the clock. I expected it would be found in some obvious place."

"Did you search for it?"

"No. I didn't take its absence seriously. The doctor told me he thought my husband had died some time between eleven and two; everything seemed quite straightforward."

"When was foul play suspected?"

"I had no suspicion at all, myself, until a young man

came to the door and asked to see me. I thought he had some appointment with my husband, and agreed to see him. It turned out that he was connected with the local paper. It appears that Irene Cobb had gone down to the office, where a friend of hers was working, and had begun a wild story about the missing clock. I told him, of course, that there was no mystery, that the death was a perfectly natural one, but that there would be an inquest, since my husband had not seen a doctor within thirteen days, the statutory time, Dr. Frensham told me, if an inquest is to be avoided."

"You had no objection to the inquest?".

"None. I expected it to be the merest formality. Colonel Hyde, the local coroner, arranged it for that afternoon."

"You anticipated no trouble?"

"None. But shortly after lunch a man came from the police station and asked me if I would mind answering some questions. He had no real right to question me, but I had nothing to hide, so I agreed. He then asked me whether I knew that my husband was contemplating altering his will. I said that he had spoken to me about it, and I had urged him to do nothing rash."

"But you hadn't been able to persuade him?"

"No."

"So that within twenty-four hours you would have been completely disinherited?"

Mrs. Ross's great golden-brown eyes stared.

"Disinherited? I? It wasn't on my account that he was proposing to alter his will, but on his son's."

"You really ask the court to believe that?" Hawkes sounded contemptuously amused.

"It's the truth. He told me that he did not mean to leave his money to be squandered by a young man whom he no longer regarded as his relation."

"He didn't tell you that he intended to cut you out also?"

"Certainly not."

"Although he had told Miss Cobb this, and also the lawyer?"

"I know nothing of that."

"Both of them are prepared to swear to that on oath!"

"I can only repeat that my husband had said nothing of this to me. In any case, as I have already told the court, I was proposing to leave him, so that I should not have inherited his money in any event."

"You had told that to no one but Harry Ross?"

"I had had no opportunity. I had only just come to that decision."

Oh, admittedly, the case against her was pretty black. She was a woman accustomed to certain standards of comfort; she was not fitted for any particular form of work and indeed would probably find it difficult to obtain any. We had only her word for it that she knew nothing of her husband's intentions. McNeile had already taken her through the history of the inquest. Hyde, who presided, was a retired R.A.M.C. man, and he had been struck by a small patch of dried blood that had clotted on one side of the dead man's mouth. This had apparently been overlooked by

Frensham who, after all, had no reason to suspect anything but natural death. Hyde, who was inclined to
fuss unduly, gave it as his belief that this blood clot
had been caused by some form of pressure. The dead
man had been found lying on his right side, and the
clot was at the left corner of the jaw. After that, events
began to move rapidly. I believe the Cobb woman
was at the bottom of the trouble; she had aroused a
lot of curiosity about the clock, that, mysteriously
enough, had not been discovered. Police examined the
room in which Teddy had been found, and discovered
a cushion, in a chair, on which was a stain of blood.
The cushion had been flung into the chair with the
stained side downward.

Hawkes was like a puppy worrying a slipper when
he got to that point. He kept tossing it away and
coming back to it until Mrs. Ross was practically exhausted. She kept on saying steadfastly that she had
no idea how the cushion could have been stained; she
tried to suggest that her husband had had toothache
and had hugged the cushion to his cheek.

"Hugged it until it bled—his cheek, I mean? That
doesn't seem very likely. Besides, if he had done that,
surely he would have washed the blood from his face
before he lay down."

"I can't offer any other explanation."

"If the cushion had been held over his face and
pressed down hard, don't you think it might have
caused the gum to bleed?"

"I don't know. Perhaps."

"Your husband suffered from pyorrhea, did he not?"

"Yes."

"So that the gums would be very tender. They would bleed easily?"

"I suppose they would."

I saw what he was driving at there. He wanted to show that even moderate pressure such as even a woman might exert would cause the gum to be bruised. Viola Ross ceded him this point; she was beginning to wear an exhausted look that might have softened any man less ruthless than Hawkes.

"Now, we come to the subject of the clock, Mrs. Ross. You are, of course, aware where it was eventually found?"

"In a hat box in my husband's room."

"Can you offer the court any explanation of its presence there?"

"If I had one I should have offered it to my own counsel long ago. Or to the police. They've asked me often enough."

"You don't suggest that your husband put it there?"

"I don't see who else could have. No one else was in the room."

"No one? Have you forgotten the cushion, Mrs. Ross?"

"I don't agree that that proves there was anyone else in the room. I think there may be a perfectly rational explanation, only I haven't thought of it yet."

"Perhaps you think there is a perfectly rational explanation of the clock in the hat box, too?"

"There must be. He must have buried it there to stop its noise. It was found jammed among his hats,

29

with a scarf wound around it."

"You've told us that your husband understood the workings of the clock?"

"He did."

"Then why didn't he simply switch it off when it began to chime?"

"Perhaps something had gone wrong."

"It has been examined by an expert, who tells us that it is in perfect order."

"Then I can't explain it at all."

"Even assuming that your husband did do any such thing, can you tell the court why, having buried the clock, he immediately got back into bed and presumably died there?"

"I can only suppose that it was some kind of mental spasm."

"Was he accustomed to these mental spasms, as you call them?"

"He had been rather strange lately, as I've told you. He would walk about talking to himself. He neglected his work, his manner was strange. Other people noticed it; they asked me what was wrong."

"It seems quite obvious what was wrong. He was anxious—"

"It was more than that. He had begun to put things in queer places, money and books, and he hid a pair of links inside his evening shoes. Dr. Frensham had spoken of a possible nervous breakdown."

"Had your husband spoken of taking a holiday?"

"No. He said he had too much to do. He was very much engaged with this primer of his."

"I see. So he pressed his own face against a cushion until it bled, he made no attempt to wash away the blood—there was no blood mark on sheets, pillow case or handkerchief—he hid the clock in the hat box, without switching off the alarm—and then lay down in bed and had a heart attack. Doesn't it strike you as strange that he made no attempt to move out of bed, to ring a bell, to call out?"

"There was no one to hear him, if he had. Martha sleeps like a corpse on the floor above."

"According to the medical evidence, he must have died practically without a struggle."

"Is that so very unusual in a case of heart disease?"

"Not very usual. Now, Mrs. Ross, I want you to look at this." He passed her an exhibit, marked "5," in a minute cellophane container. "Will you look at that and tell us what you think it is?"

"It looks like a stone out of a ring."

"It is a stone out of a ring, a very small diamond, what is called a chip. Now, I understand that you have an opal ring set in very small diamonds, that you habitually wear."

"I have, of course. It's a very ordinary setting."

"The diamonds approximate to the one in your hand."

"Yes."

"I believe there is a diamond missing from your setting."

"There is."

"Do you remember how long it has been missing?"

"I couldn't say."

31

"Probably you would notice if it had been missing for some time."

"I might not. They are so very small."

"Still, it's reasonable to suppose you would notice. And in fact, you had not?"

"No."

"But you admit the absence of a stone now?"

"Yes."

"Mrs. Ross, that stone you have in your hand fits perfectly the vacant place in your ring. That stone was found in your husband's bed."

"I can only suppose it had become loose and fell out while I was bending over him trying to awaken him the next morning."

"You admit that you did not employ much energy trying to rouse him, that you realized almost at once that he was beyond help?"

"When a stone becomes loose the smallest exertion will shake it out of its socket."

Oh, she fought him blow for blow, but slowly he was wearing her down. The clock, the cushion, the ring. . . . And she had to admit that there had been a disturbance that day on her return from a visit to town.

"You had been to see your stepson?"

"Yes."

"To take him money?"

"Only a very little. Chiefly to tell him that I couldn't help him any more, and to warn him that his father was proposing to disinerit him."

"You told him that?"

"I thought it fair to warn him."

"What good would that do?"

"He might have thought it worth while coming down to see his father."

"And did he?"

"Not so far as I know."

"You have not been in touch with your stepson after your husband's death?"

"I telephoned to him on the morning of the fifth, but he was out. I left a message and later he telephoned to me. He came down later in the day."

"He, of course, could throw no light on the mystery?"

"Of course not. He hadn't seen his father for months."

"Did your husband know that you had visited Harry Ross that day?"

"Yes."

"And he was displeased?"

"Yes."

"Did he suggest that you had your own reasons for visiting him?"

"I have told you my reasons."

"That is not an answer to my question. I have to ask you to tell the court whether your husband believed you had other reasons for visiting Harry Ross."

"He had no grounds for any other suspicion."

Here the judge intervened. "You must answer the question, Mrs. Ross."

She flung back her head. "If he chose to suspect that I had any romantic attachment for his son he was quite wrong. I was a great deal older than he. The notion was absurd."

33

"Nevertheless, he did suspect some such situation?"

"He pretended he did."

"He had hinted at such suspicions before that day? When he forbade your visits, for instance?"

"I shouldn't allow myself to be swayed by anything so—vile." How her voice rose on that last word, so that it throbbed through the court. Hawkes, however, was quite unmoved. He went on asking her how often she had been at Harry's rooms? Hadn't she thought it indiscreet? Wasn't it true that he was a very attractive young man? Hadn't he changed his address some time after she began visiting him? Wasn't it a fact that his first landlady had objected to a lodger receiving visits from a married woman? With every word he spoke Hawkes was trying to put before the jury the picture of an unfaithful wife, threatened with disgrace, with poverty, with disaster. I looked at the faces around me. They were hardening into conviction. Hawkes' face was assuming a look I have sometimes seen upon the faces of hunting men; a gloating look. He was without pity and without decency.

He let her go at last with a final question that completed his case.

"Mrs. Ross, I've only one more thing to ask you. Would you—could you—say that your life with your husband was happy?"

He had her in a corner there, and they both knew it. You could have heard a pin drop in the court.

"No," she said at last in a low clear voice. "It was not happy—but I did not kill him all the same."

"And—he was aware of your unhappiness? You had

told him you hated being married to him?"

She seemed to sag as though she had put every atom of energy and courage into her last speech; for the first time her eyes implored him. Presently, under that pitiless glare, she found her voice.

"I don't know," she said weakly. "I simply don't know."

"Come, come, Mrs. Ross, this is absurd. You must be aware whether you had told your husband that you wished you had never married him."

"One says so many things," she whispered.

"But not things like that very often, surely."

Here, mercifully, the judge intervened. Leaning forward, he addressed the prisoner: "Mrs. Ross, if you don't remember, it is impossible for you to answer that question. Nor are you required to do so."

I saw Hawkes' face close up till it hadn't a grain of expression in it. But there was a look in his eyes that boded her no good. After all, even if the judge had intervened, he had done what he had set out to do. He had given the court—so much was obvious to us all—the impression that he was examining a guilty woman.

McNeile didn't dare press her much further; she was at the end of her tether and he knew it. He did what he could to dissipate the general atmosphere of hostility, but he wasn't particularly successful.

He called his other witnesses. Harry Ross—but he didn't ask him much. It wasn't safe. Harry was a good looking fellow, dark, resolute in manner, but clearly apprehensive. His answers dovetailed all right with

Viola Ross's, but I doubt if that helped her very much. A good many people thought they'd put up their defense together. Hawkes had the last word before the judge summed up, and, as the man behind me leaned forward to mutter in my ear, it was all over but the shouting.

THREE

"IT LOOKS pretty black to me," said Morrison in a gloomy voice. "I don't see how they can hope to prove beyond doubt that she did it, but if she didn't, who the devil did?"

"All evidence in a murder trial is bound to be circumstantial," said the woman, whose name was Bates. "People don't make a point of committing murder with witnesses to testify against them."

"Couldn't some one have broken into the house while she was out?" suggested Chalmers hopefully.

"Who?" asked the Bates woman.

"We don't know. After all, most people's private lives are pretty well a sealed book to their neighbors. He may have had enemies."

"Who admitted the murderer? The excellent Martha?"

That floored us. You simply couldn't conceive of Martha being in a plot to smother Teddy.

"I suppose there's no possibility of doubt that it was murder? Accident is absolutely out of court?"

"Absolutely," we assured the speaker. "They've had two doctors on the case. There can't be any question. Besides, what about the clock?"

"It's damned mysterious," we agreed.

"To my mind it isn't mysterious at all. Mrs. Ross knew that the clock would go off at midnight; she didn't know how to work it; she knew that her husband would waken at the first sound. Clearly, she was up in his room for some purpose—possibly he had some evidence against her that she knew she must have—he showed signs of waking—she snatched up the clock and wrapped it in a shawl, and then, when she realized she must be discovered, she seized the cushion and held it over his face. You can't get away from the stone in the ring that was found in his bed."

"There is an alternative explanation," I urged stubbornly. "I don't see why she shouldn't be telling the truth. Besides, if she put the clock in the hat box, why didn't she take it out again afterwards?"

"Because she forgot about it, of course. On second thought, I should say she wrapped the clock up and put it away before it was due to strike. Then she began her search. Probably she realized she was ruined and the thought came to her how helpless he was—he was a little man, you know, and he can't have looked much larger than a sparrow in bed—and she acted on impulse. She's a powerful woman."

"It's all speculation," demurred Morrison.

"Well, some one murdered him," declared Miss Bates.

"It doesn't seem to me we've got any facts worth

mentioning," said a worried little voice, recalling the Gnat in *Through the Looking-Glass*. "No one saw her go into her husband's room, no one saw her come out. They didn't find her fingerprints on the clock— yes, I know the shawl would rub them off, but the fact remains there weren't any; she sent for a doctor at once, she didn't mind a bit about the inquest. She rang up her stepson quite openly and left a message with his landlady. It all seems to me too much above-board to be true."

"That's her cunning," said Miss Bates, with finality.

"I simply don't see how we can find her guilty," continued the voice.

"Then do we assume that Edward Ross smothered himself?"

"No, of course not. He was murdered by some person or persons unknown."

"Why didn't she replace the clock?" I asked again.

"She probably forgot that." Two or three voices answered me at once. "They say every murderer makes one slip."

"If it hadn't been for that secretary person, probably no one would have mentioned the clock."

"She had a chance of getting the clock out of the box later," I suggested.

"Had she? I doubt it. She looked in the room where it should have been, and the doctor and Miss Cobb helped. Then Miss Cobb herself says she searched in the library, and Martha helped. They looked every-where. If Mrs. Ross had suddenly produced it, she'd have to have explained where she got it from. It might be safer to leave it in the box for the present."

"She could have chucked it out of the window," I suggested. "There was a garden outside."

"You forget. It rained in the morning, a regular soaker. If she'd pitched the clock out after the doctor came it would have landed in the mud, and everyone would have known it hadn't been there before the rain started. One thing about this spate of detectives stories," continued the speaker chattily, "it does warn you of all the things you mustn't do."

"It would take a policeman to find a clock in a hat box," observed Morrison heavily. "It's like G. K. Chesterton—you don't look in a sideboard for a hamadryad, because you don't expect to find hamadryads in sideboards."

"If nobody else got in," said a man who hadn't spoken before, "and it doesn't seem likely that anyone did, then she must have done it."

We argued the possibility of Martha being involved, but we had to give that up. Apart from the manifest absurdity of such a woman having an affair with a man like Teddy Ross, there wasn't a grain of motive. She had been in his employ before his second marriage, he paid her well, she gained nothing by murdering him. You simply couldn't frame a case against her. Not that I wanted to do that. I simply wanted to get Viola Ross acquitted, and it looked to me as though it was going to prove an uncommonly difficult job.

"If there's the barest possibility, no matter how improbable, that any one else could have done it, you ought to acquit her," said I.

"Is there a shadow of doubt?" asked Miss Bates. "Clocks don't put themselves into hat boxes."

"There's never been any suggestion that the servant did it," Morrison cried. "We've got to determine whether, in the opinion of us all, Mrs. Ross did it. Well, if she didn't, who did? That's the crux of the problem."

"She had motive, opportunity, sufficient muscular strength . . . she admitted she was miserable with her husband. . . ."

"If that's going to be allowed to count as a motive for murder, there's going to be an orgy for coffin-makers," I said.

The Gnat's voice was heard again. "You must take it into account all the same. We can't say that she was having a love affair with her stepson, but the fact does remain that she visited him several times at his lodgings after her husband had forbidden it. He didn't put up a very good show either. He was afraid of something."

"Afraid of seeing her condemned for murder, very likely."

"He seemed to me more afraid that something might come out."

Back and forth we went, weighing this trifle and that, stressing first one point and then another. It looked to me as though we might be there all night. I thanked my stars that in this country a majority verdict in a case of murder isn't enough to secure sentence of death. It's got to be unanimous. And I was resolved to hold out till the Judgment Day. I might not be able to sway them, but I could force a retrial, and in the meanwhile I could work—and work—

We reached the stage where eleven of the jury were prepared to vote guilty. I hung out for an acquittal.

"You don't care whether she murdered her husband or not. You just want her to get off," the horse-faced woman accused me.

"I want to be more sure," I reiterated. I said the same thing to all the others.

The judge sent in a message to say that if we required his help, it was at our disposal. The court was half empty when at last we returned. I suppose people couldn't stay half the night even when there was a woman's life at stake. The usual things had to be done, meals prepared, houses cared for. This drama of Viola Ross's fate was only an atom in the great moving pageant; it mattered to hardly anyone, except as a sensation, and then only to a tiny minority. I couldn't help wondering, as we waited and argued, what she was thinking, how she felt, sitting hour after hour with the matron in the cell behind the court. Did she have any premonition how the case would go? I looked at her once as they brought her back and then looked away. Every atom of color and vitality had drained out of her face. It must be pretty awful, waiting in an endless silence. During the trial there had been the stir of life, the evidence of one witness after another, attention to be focused, and that general atmosphere of a court when a capital charge is being tried, that is as definite as a wind blowing. But for the hours of suspense there can be no amelioration.

The usual question was asked. "Members of the jury, are you agreed on your verdict?"

Morrison said, "I regret to say we have one dissentient."

The judge inquired whether he thought there would be any value in reconsidering the case, but Morrison said not. It was now so late that to remain any longer would mean being locked up for the night, and I was as resolved to continue to vote for an acquittal as my colleagues to find Viola Ross guilty. The judge was a philosopher. He accepted the situation, addressed the court, dismissed it. Miss Bates was purple with fury. "Thank Heaven you can't serve on the next jury," she cried at me.

Next morning all the papers carried headlines.

"Cathedral Town Murder Case: Sensation," they said. And, "Ross Case: Jury Disagree." Already one enterprising journal had an article, "The Twelfth Man." I glanced through it, almost expecting to see my own name. I picked up the house telephone and ordered breakfast at once. I knew it would be no time before the local reporters would be gathering on my doorstep like vultures around a corpse; and pretty soon the London reporters would join them. I decided to go up to town and lie low for some days. It wouldn't help the plans I was formulating to have my footsteps dogged by a pack of amateur sleuths all anxious to know what I was going to do next, all ready to pin a romantic story on to my feeling about Mrs. Ross's innocence, all raising obstacles on every side.

I had not started, however, when my telephone rang

and I was told that Miss Cobb wanted to see me. I cursed her heartily.

"Will you say I have an urgent appointment in town?"

There was a pause. Then the porter said, "Are you going up on the 9.40?"

"I daren't miss it."

"The lady says that's all right. She'll be on that, too."

I groaned and gave in. "Send her in," I said. "But warn her I only have a few minutes."

She came in, looking the color of death; she had jammed an unbecoming straw hat on her head, and I should say she was a girl who never used make-up.

"So it was you," she greeted me melodramatically. "Why did you do it?"

I looked at her with dislike. "Will you tell me what you want, bursting into my room like this?" I asked. "I've told you I have to go to town."

"I shouldn't think you'd be wise. Half the place knows it was you and they all want to know why."

"Because I didn't consider the evidence permitted any other verdict," I told her. "You might tell your inquisitive friends that, if they ask."

"What good have you done her? She'll only have to stand another trial, and it isn't likely she'll get someone infatuated with her on the next jury."

"That's no concern of mine," I returned, as coolly as I could, wishing I could sling the wretched creature out, neck and crop.

"I suppose you didn't think of him at all," she argued.

"I was there to consider the verdict."

"You know she was guilty."

"If I'd believed that I'd have agreed with the other eleven jurors. By the way, how do you know I was the dissenter?"

"Miss Bates told me."

"Ah! She's a friend of yours?"

"I have a room in the same house. Of course, she says it's infamous. Naturally, Mrs. Ross wanted her husband out of the way."

"Just a minute," I said. "Is there anyone you hate?"

"Mrs. Ross," said she between her teeth.

"Ah, yes. You didn't think her good enough for her husband."

"She wasn't fit to black his boots." You know the type of woman who goes all hysterical on you all of a sudden.

"But you don't propose to murder her?"

"You don't murder everybody you loathe."

"Yet you suggested that she murdered her husband."

"I know she did. She had everything—motive, opportunity. . . . Don't tell me she was going to like being poor and a disgrace. Besides, she had her lover to think of."

I caught the woman by the shoulders. "Look here," said I. "That's slander. Even the prosecution never established the existence of a lover, though God knows they tried hard enough."

"I don't care what they established. Nobody doubts that she had one. All you mean is, she's been clever and not left any proof lying about."

45

"I suppose you could even supply his name," I said.

"Harry Ross," returned she sullenly.

"Have you an atom of proof?"

"She went to his rooms, she was alone with him there, they wrote letters—nobody knows what was in them— she was giving him money—he'd been turned out of his father's house. . . . "

"Not on her account."

"How do we know? Besides, I'll tell you something. Mr. Ross had got proof."

I looked up, startled but disbelieving. "Oh, yes?"

"Yes. It came the day he died. He told me about it."

"What did he say?"

" 'Well, my fine couple, I've got you now.' "

Just the sort of thing Teddy Ross would say, I told myself.

"What did he mean by that?"

"He had a letter."

"Who from?"

"I don't know. He didn't show it to me."

"Why not, if you were so much in his confidence?"

"He didn't discuss his private affairs with me. I shouldn't have expected it. I shouldn't even have liked it."

"Then how can you be so sure?"

"He asked me a lot of rather queer questions."

"What about?"

"Well, actually about Mrs. Ross's movements."

"You didn't tell the court all this."

"I tried to, but they shut me up. I couldn't actually produce the letter, you see."

"Where is it now then?"

"I expect she destroyed it."

"Having murdered him first?"

"I dare say she couldn't have got hold of it any other way."

"It doesn't occur to you that she might have preferred the divorce court, supposing it was to come to that, to standing her trial for murder?"

"There was the money. She was greedy for money and she didn't want to work. I know!"

"I don't see how you can say that," I protested.

"Wasn't I in and out of that house for months? I had plenty of time to observe."

"She worked before her marriage."

"And married the first man who asked her. No, if she'd wanted to work she'd have saved her husband the expense of a secretary. But he used to say she didn't take the slightest interest in his book."

"Either you have a mathematical mind or you haven't. Very likely she hadn't. I haven't myself."

"I don't know why you're so keen to get her off, unless you're like Lord Peter Wimsey, who was so much intrigued by meeting a murderess that he proposed at once."

"She doesn't happen to be a murderess. And as for marrying Mrs. Ross—the idea is fantastic." Well, so it was.

"Well, it's very odd you taking so much trouble if you don't."

"She's a human being. I want to prevent a great injustice being done."

"You're very sure it is an injustice."

"I was elected to serve on the jury in order that I might give my genuine point of view. I don't think they've proved the case against her."

Miss Cobb sniffed. "I don't know how much more proof you want. She goes up to town for the day, comes back about five o'clock—has a tremendous row with her husband. . . . "

"How do you know that?" I interrupted. "Were you there? I thought you had a job."

"I'd been told I could get off early because there wasn't much for me to do. I got to The Laurels a little after half-past four. It was then that Mr. Ross began to talk."

"And I suppose you heard everything they said to one another?"

"You know I didn't. I was in the dining room. Mr. Ross asked me to wait. But presently Mrs. Ross came slamming out and she went out at once."

"She said in her evidence she didn't go out till after dinner."

"That was later. She went out as soon as he left the library."

"That's news," I said. "Where do you suppose she went?"

"I haven't any doubt at all, only here again I can't prove anything. I know she went to telephone to him."

"To . . . "

"To Harry Ross. She wanted to warn him."

"That her husband had discovered all?" I was intentionally melodramatic.

Irene Cobb flushed angrily. "Oh, you can laugh, but I bet you that's what she did do. It's only a toll call to London, and he could get down here in a little over an hour."

"You suggest he was down here that night?" I hadn't thought of that.

"I don't suppose they'd discuss that sort of thing over the phone."

"And when she went to the pictures—but, of course, you don't think she did go to the pictures."

"We know she went to the pictures. She made a point of being seen there. She knew she might need to give evidence. But we don't know how long she stayed there. And though she arrived alone it doesn't mean she left alone."

"Pretty risky walking out with a man as well known to the neighborhood as Harry Ross."

"It would be safe enough if they walked out in the middle of the last big picture. No one would be coming in then. Or they could have come out separately and made their arrangements. Then he'd go back to town."

"And leave her to commit the murder?"

"I should say the murder was her idea. Besides it would be much safer for her to do it. She'd be in the house, you see; she knew he wouldn't wake till about twelve—he'd set the alarm for eleven forty-five —she says she came back at eleven-thirty—it's all obvious enough."

It sounded worse than ever, and my determination to get Mrs. Ross acquitted strengthened. Also I began to lose my temper. "I don't quite know what you expected to gain by coming to see me."

"I hoped to make you see how stupid it is to try and prove that Mrs. Ross is innocent. You're only prolonging the agony."

"That ought to please you."

"I just came in to see if I could persuade you to stop this—this absurd campaign," she went on. "If you don't want to marry her, I can't see what you're doing it for. Anyhow, I warn you, I shall do everything in my power to hinder you."

"I'm sure you will," I said, understanding the motives that prompt men to instinctive murder, and I bowed her out.

After she had gone I stood thinking for some time. I realized that she was quite right. Everybody would suggest that I was working for Mrs. Ross for some romantic motive; actually, I hadn't any intention of marrying her. I had some time ago seen the girl I wanted to marry. She was young and, while not precisely unsophisticated, had a kind of bloom that you don't easily find in a girl nowadays. Her father was a rich man, owner of The Towers, and had refused to agree to an engagement until I was in a position to support a wife in reasonable comfort. Now I wondered whether it would be wise to declare myself openly, explain my interest in the Ross affair, and take the risk of being called a fortune hunter. It seemed to me that Bunty herself might be my best guide here.

I could not call at The Towers before ten o'clock, but just after that hour I arrived. London, I decided, could wait. In the hall I met Colonel Friar.

"Making yourself pretty conspicuous," he growled.

I knew then that Miss Bates had spread her poisonous yarn all around the town.

"I'm sorry about that, sir," I said, "but I have a conscience of my own."

"H'm. It's a pity this woman hasn't."

"I really called to see Bunty," I ventured.

"Didn't imagine you came for the pleasure of my company. All the same, there's something I want to say to you. It's about Bunty," he added over his shoulder, leading the way into the room called the den.

My heart sank. As soon as he had shut the door the colonel swung around and said, "Look here, I understand from my girl that you're hanging about after her."

"I hope to be in a position to ask her to marry me quite shortly," I returned, nettled by his manner.

"On what?"

"On what I earn as a novelist."

"And what's that?"

"I make about eight hundred a year at present."

"And you consider that an adequate figure on which to support my daughter?"

"Men live on less."

"But there's more than that," he went on belligerently. "I understand you're involving yourself with this Mrs. Ross."

"I realize it's not a popular subject with you, sir."

"Popular?" He threw back his head and his nostrils quivered, as though he were really going to spout flame at me. "Let me tell you this, sir. Unless you drop this crazy notion at once I shall forbid my daughter to see you altogether."

That sort of thing may have gone down all right at the beginning of the century, when perhaps there was a spiritless type of young man who allowed himself to suffer dictation, but it set up every hackle I possess.

"Bunty's of age," I reminded him, "and, in any case she would be the last person to want me to abandon an affair like this knowing how strongly I feel about it."

The door flashed open before he could reply, and Bunty was with us.

"Oh, Richard, I heard you'd come." She stood looking from her father to me.

"I wanted to see you, most particularly, before I go to town," said I, taking the bull by the horns.

"To town?"

"Yes. I have to see a lawyer in connection with Mrs. Ross's defense."

"You're defending her?"

"I must do what I can. I'd never have an easy moment again if I didn't."

"Because you think she didn't do it."

"So far as it's possible for mortal man who wasn't actually on the spot to assert such a thing, I know she didn't do it."

"Feller's singularly infatuated," growled the colonel,

determined not to leave us alone.

"Infatuated by a conviction perhaps," I agreed. "Bunty, you do see my point?"

Bunty behaved like an angel. "Of course, I see, if you feel like that, Richard, you couldn't just do nothing about it. I was wondering . . . "

"Well?" My heart was beating a tattoo against my ribs.

"Whether I could do anything to help."

"Bunty!" thundered the colonel, and, "You darling!" said I.

Bunty took no notice of her father's gurglings. She came across and put her hands on my shoulders. "I know how you feel. I believe in you. I hope you'll find out the truth—whatever it is."

"I've warned you, if you go on with this affair you'll have nothing to do with my daughter. Mary," he only called her that in moments of great stress, "you hear me?"

"That's blackmail," said Bunty calmly. "And I wouldn't want to marry any man who could be silenced like that."

"There's no talk of your marrying him."

"We've often talked about it."

"Not to me." He was purple with rage.

"Well, father dear, what was the use when you simply called him a fortune hunter? As if people care nowadays who provides the money. There's more to life than just that."

"Most of the other things can only be bought with money. You heard what I said, Bunty?"

Bunty gave him a long, cool stare. "All right. Then we'll live on Richard's earnings. I've always thought I should run a divine house, and it'll be less work having two rooms than ten."

It wasn't surprising I wanted to marry her.

I left the house with the colonel's words ringing in my ears. "I mean what I say. You won't like making your income clothe two instead of one. I know your sort." I thought it uncommonly probable that he did mean what he said. I knew he wanted Bunty to marry young Denis Markham, and Denis was keen enough. Bunty had quite liked him at one time; I'd had hard work to make her notice my existence. Father and mother, too, might work on her to bring her back to her first fancy. But all the same, I told myself grimly, as I took a ticket for London, I couldn't let that stop me. I wasn't going to let anything stop me. Even if I knew going on with the case involved a permanent rupture with Bunty I was going on. I had to. I felt as strongly as that about it.

FOUR

In London I went to see a man I know called Crook, a lawyer of some repute, though not, his enemies are inclined to assert, always the most enviable repute. He was a tub of a man with a big inquiring nose and as unscrupulous—some said—as a weasel. Any job was his meat, provided the case interested him. His best known name was the Criminal's Hope, and more than once the police had tried to pump him for information about certain notorious East End gangs.

His name, as I have said, was connected with quite a number of queer cases; but he had been remarkably successful where people with less blemished reputations had failed. He was mixed-up, for instance, in the Chinese Gallery affair down at Plenders, and when most of the world was saying that Horsley, the M.P., had smothered his wife, Crook stepped in there, too. He didn't worry over the niceties of a case, but if it appealed to him he took it on, and he'd hang on till grim death. I don't say he ever actually tampered with the evidence, but he had an amazing way of twisting it to suit his own convenience.

"Not had enough of the law?" he greeted me. "I hope they gave you spiral springs in your cell."

"It wasn't as bad as that," I told him, "we weren't locked up for the night."

"No thanks to you by all accounts."

"News travels fast," said I.

Crook grinned. "I'll tell you something else," he said. "You're here to see me on that woman's account."

"That was an easy one. Why else should I be coming?"

"Never can tell. You might be in a bit of trouble of your own. It happens to the best people, and a female client told me only yesterday that we're here to help one another. She wore an emerald and black-striped woollen dress, and red hair," he added meditatively, "and she painted the emotions. For her own sake I hope she was more successful with them than with her own complexion. What do you want me to do?"

"I want to prevent a second trial, if I can. We all have our breaking point, and unless I'm much mistaken that woman's precious near hers."

"And you'd like me to provide you with a nice little dose of poison to push through the bars? You've come to the wrong shop, haven't you?"

"I believe I'm the one person in England who believes her innocent," said I.

"And you're asking me to prove it? You pay a pretty compliment, Arnold."

"Can't truth always be proved?" I demanded passionately.

"Tell that to the theologians and see what you get."

"It's got to be in this case. Call me anything you damn' well please, but the thought of that woman going to the scaffold is intolerable to me."

"What do you expect me to do at this stage? Manufacture evidence?"

"If you can fake anything that'll throw dust in the judge's eyes, by all means."

Then he said what two women had said to me already. "You don't really care whether she did it or not, do you? Well, nor for the matter of that, do I."

"You don't, eh?"

Crook winked. "What do you suppose lawyers are for?" he asked me. "To preserve equity? Don't you believe it. They exist to get people out of tight corners, and the tighter the corner the higher the fee. And no one's in a tighter corner than the man who's guilty. When they talk of a reign of perfection I begin to shiver in my shoes. I see myself lining up at the Relief Office. When I hear of a case like this, where it's all Lombard Street to a china orange against the verdict being a favorable one, then I begin to scent money for jam."

"You're a cold blooded brute," I objected.

"Not a bit of it. I'm just an average business man."

"Do you think she did it?" I demanded.

Crook waved that aside. "What I believe, old boy, don't matter a row of pins. It's what you can make the jury believe. And you can't·lobby with a jury—you've got to convince 'em, against their better natures if need be. Now then, where do you begin?"

"With the fact that I'm convinced of her innocence."

"That won't sway the judge, and you won't be given a chance to work on the feelings of the next jury. Any sort of proof?"

"Not yet. Just a sort of hunch."

"What's called in legal circles, a prejudice. Well, it's all one to me. What alternatives can you offer?"

"I've been taking the facts. Mrs. Ross went out about nine-fifteen. She sets the time by the fact that she met the postman at the gate, and that's his regular hour for calling. She went to the local movie, and got back sometime after eleven, say eleven-twenty or thereabouts. That means she was out of the house about two hours. During that time the only people in the house were Ross himself and an elderly maid who is deaf, and in any case went to bed at ten. So that for an hour the house was virtually empty. Any one may have come in unseen."

"The Ross house bein' like Ali Baba's cave—you've only got to say Open Sesame, and the door swings wide?"

"There may be other means of entry. Someone may have had a latchkey."

"Who, for instance?"

"I was thinking of the son. You know what Sherlock Holmes said."

"About eliminatin' all the impossibles and takin' whatever's left, however improbable, as the only answer? Yes, I know. I'm thinkin' of havin' that put up over my desk. It'll save a lot of trouble. It must be nearly as popular as 'Laugh and the world laughs with you.' Well?"

"The only other person, so far as I know, who's got a motive, is Harry Ross."

"The son, who was also being disinherited?"

"That's right."

"How does he account for his evening?"

"I don't think he's been asked. The police didn't appear to find any trace of a violent entry. I think myself they made up their minds Mrs. Ross did it."

"Lucky you aren't in Germany. You'd get three days' concentration camp for that. Are you proposin' I shall tackle Master Ross?"

"I thought you might find out something about his private affairs, whether he needed money badly, and so on. It would be easier for me to appear in the open, and it'll act as a barrage for you."

"Think of everything, don't you? What's your special idea in putting him on his guard?"

"I didn't think of it precisely like that. I thought I might ask him to help me with the job of clearing his stepmother. If he's guilty he'll jump at the idea, if only to keep in with me and realize what I'm doing."

"That's sound," Crook agreed. "And while you're distractin' him, we can try and slip a knife in his back. Of course, the idea has points. He'd know the lie of the house. How did he know it would be empty?"

"Perhaps he didn't know. I'm not suggesting premeditated murder. I've never committed a murder myself, but I imagine it's only a last resort when more peaceful methods have failed. Young Ross knew that his father was proposing to alter his will the next day and cut him out . . ."

"How did he know that?"

"Mrs. Ross had warned him. She'd been up in London that day. It wouldn't be any use for Harry to write to his father; Teddy Ross would probably have pitched the letter unopened on the fire. In any case, it wouldn't have made him change his mind. He may have hoped that at a personal interview. . . . "

"Speakin' as a lawyer, I'm all against the personal interview," interjected Crook.

"But then Harry Ross isn't a lawyer. Besides, it was probably his last chance."

"I see you've thought it all out. Carry on. Why didn't he phone his father?"

"Because Teddy would have refused to speak to him. He told him he need never darken his doors again."

"That'll sound well in court. Of course, as things stand, the son inherits."

"They both inherit."

"A person found guilty on a capital charge cannot inherit. However, I get your point. There's equal motive. In fact, the son may have a greater motive. What were his relations with his stepmother?"

"Malice says disreputable."

"But no proof?"

"Unless you count her going to his rooms on three or four occasions."

"And he's doin' journalism? And not very successful journalism at that."

"That's so."

"I don't imagine his room would be the ideal meetin'-place. Well, well, evil, like beauty, is in the eye of the beholder. You'd think she might have had more sense, though."

"Surely the fact that she went there openly . . . "

"With her husband's knowledge?"

"N-no."

"Couldn't she write?"

"Her correspondence was being severely censored."

"There are post boxes in town."

"Teddy might have bought in the hag who keeps the lodgings."

"He might. After all, mathematics were his strong suit. What's the son's opinion?"

"I don't think he's given it actually. I suppose if he were violently partisan—on Mrs. Ross's side, I mean—he might arouse suspicion."

"And by doing nothing he also seems to have aroused suspicion? Well, well, you can't hope to please everyone. And naturally you'd rather believe it was Harry Ross than the lady."

"I don't know Harry particularly well, but I can't believe she's the type."

"Don't talk to me about types where women are concerned. They're all individuals. 'The world is a bundle of hay, And women the asses who pull, Each pulls in a different way. . . . ' Fill in the last line, as it suits you. Well, Ross went down to see his father. Who let him in? Not Martha, or she'd have said so. You're not suggesting Ross Senior came down, let him in and then went meekly back to bed, and allowed himself to be smothered?"

"Of course not. Mind you, I don't say you'll get

a clear case against him. But you might get up enough doubt to get her acquitted."

"That's the first sensible thing you've said," remarked Crook rudely.

"Though, naturally it would be better still if we could put someone else in her place."

"On the drop, in short. Quite the bright boy, aren't you? Well, you say your piece and we'll hang about behind the scenes. But don't suppose this is a competition. For the Lord's sake, keep in touch with us, and don't think you're Charlie Chan, and can teach us our job, because you can't." As I reached the door he added casually, "This ends in orange blossom, I take it, if all goes well?"

I began to understand Colonel Friar's attitude, and to thank my stars that Bunty was the right kind of a girl.

Harry Ross was not in when I arrived at his lodgings. The house was drab, dark, respectable and cheap. It was in the once genteel neighborhood of Bayswater, but the back looked over a coal-yard and the front over an arid oblong of intermittent grass and sooty laurels inaccurately called a square. While I was inquiring of the landlady the probable time of Harry's return a square set, bespectacled young man ascended the four tesselated steps and proceeded to take charge of the situation.

"May be back in five minutes or not till midnight," he told me succinctly. "Never can tell with these writing johnnies. Sometimes he has an all night session and sometimes he's lounging in and out of the house half the day. Isn't that right, Mrs. Judges"

Mrs. Judges said sourly that it was. "I like a gentleman to have a proper job," she told us. "I didn't understand how it was when Mr. Ross took a room here. I'm not accustomed to my lodgers hanging about half the day looking for a job. Next thing it'll be the dole."

"Not with Mr. Ross," the young man assured her.

"Only because he hasn't got enough stamps," she flashed. "Well, will you come back or what?"

I hesitated. I didn't much care for this unappreciative welcome. "Come up to my room and wait there," the young man offered. "I dare say he won't be long."

"Doing journalism, isn't he?" said I, not because I wanted to know, but because there was always the chance, remote though it might appear, that he might be able to help me.

"He is. And a fool thing to do, too, if you ask me. Too much talking in the world as it is, and all this talking on paper as well—where does it get you to? Motors now . . . "

"Your job, I suppose?"

"That's right." He told me about himself as he moved about the room. He worked in a garage. He knew Ross, though not intimately.

"Seems a bit under the weather. Not too popular with Ma Judges either. I believe she'd have told him his room was wanted if it hadn't been for all this stink about Mrs. Ross. You've read the case, I expect."

"It's my part of the world," I said.

"Rotten affair, anyhow. Ma Judges is as pleased as

Punch. She said she always knew the woman was up to no good."

"What did she know about her?"

"She used to come here to see Ross. I don't think Ma ever believed she was his stepmother. Well, she's convinced of that anyhow, but she's got a dirty mind, that woman." He said it quite tolerantly. "Wants something to cheer her up after keeping a drunken husband for fourteen years and her own head above water for about forty. I heard her talking to the woman the day the husband was found dead. She was like a cat nosing something suspicious."

"How do you mean—talking to her? She wasn't up here."

"No, but she telephoned Ross quite early to give him the news. And he wasn't in. I met him, as it happens, stepping off the train on my way down."

"What earthly time would that be?"

"Just before nine. Been on an all night job, perhaps. These newspaper men do sometimes."

"It must have been a bit of a shock for him," I ventured.

"There wasn't much love lost between them, I fancy. Old man Ross had practically disowned him. Darned shame, you know, just because he wanted to follow his bent, even if it was a pretty queer sort of bent. No, I don't think he would have minded much about the old man if he'd passed out in the usual way. But he was pretty cut up about his stepmother being taken for the job."

"She'd been very good to him," I said.

Kenward looked down his nose. "A chap of his age oughtn't to need women, even if they are their father's second wives, to be good to them," he said doggedly.

I asked lightly, "Did his stepmother come here often?"

"I only saw her once, though I believe she came several times. Grand looking woman. Some men have all the luck. Whether she did it or not I'm sorry for her having to face another trial."

"Unless something fresh comes to light that puts a new complexion on the affair, there's no alternative."

"That's a bit improbable, isn't it, after so long?"

"Remember the Gutteridge case? They were six months getting their man there."

I waited a long time, but at last I left a message that I'd come back after dinner. I wondered how much Crook would find out, how far he would expect me to go. I knew he loathed interference. He thought most people incompetent, and it was a favor my being allowed to have anything to do with the affair.

"The lay mind!" he'd say. "The lay mind! God help it. Thinks we do all our work by rule of three and wants to be allowed to play with us. Like a kid trying to make pastry." All the same he had given me some good advice.

"Give a guilty man plenty of rope and you can trust him to make his own noose. It's so hard to believe that what's known to you isn't equally obvious to the next man. It isn't everyone who's got the sense of the fellow who left an important letter turned inside out in his letter rack while they bored holes in the seats of his chairs hunting for it. Mostly they take such precautions to shield 'emselves they attract attention in a way they'd never do if they had the sense to keep their mouths shut. Like the lady lapwing that makes such a tamarsha when you get near her nest you know you're warm, while the odds are you'd have missed it if you'd been hunting for it."

FIVE

When I got back to young Ross's room after dinner, I found him in and expecting me.

"Kenward told me you were asking for me," he said. "He didn't tell me why. Only something about my stepmother."

"You do remember me, of course, though we have met so little of recent years." I offered him my hand.

"Of course," said he, not particularly graciously.

"I was the dissenting juryman," I explained.

"The deuce you were! I hadn't thought of that. But how do you think I can help you?" He fished out a cigarette case and offered it to me.

"I don't know that you can. I suppose if you could have done anything definite you'd have come forward before this—or perhaps you believe Mrs. Ross is guilty."

He snapped the cigarette shut. "What the hell do I care if she was guilty or not? Oh, I know he was my father, but my God! you don't know how narrow, how intolerable, he could be. He had the power of the purse, and he used it. Made us both realize we were pretty helpless against that. Not that he could stop

67

me coming up here, but he saw to it that I should go as damned short as possible. I suppose you think this place is pretty awful, but it's nothing compared with some of the places I've lived during the last twelve months."

"What the devil do you expect me to do?" he went on.

"Did your father have any enemies you know of?" I asked. It was an absurd question and I knew it.

"None who'd want to murder him. The game wouldn't be worth the candle."

"Mrs. Ross may easily have thought that, too."

"Quite, but you've got to make a court believe that."

"Do you mean to tell me seriously that you believe she was the kind of woman who could smother her husband?"

He didn't seem to know where to look. He stared from wall to wall, from a lithograph of kittens in a basket to an enormous framed print of a lovely lady with a lionskin flung casually around one shoulder, and a troup of tigers eyeing her hungrily.

"Oh, God," he cried at last, "I don't know what to think. I've been half crazy ever since the affair started. At first, of course, I didn't believe it. But what other answer is there? He couldn't have smothered himself. And there's the stone from her ring and the blood on the pillow. You can't ignore them—or explain them, except as eleven-twelfths of the jury have already done."

"There was a maid there. . . . "

"You can't suspect Martha!" He laughed abruptly. "He hadn't even left her a legacy."

"And nobody else had a latchkey?"

"I had one while I was there, but my father took it before I left."

"Then he might have given it to someone else."

"He might—but who—unless it was Irene Cobb. But she'd never murder him. She thought he was marvelous."

"What did he think of her?" I asked.

"Oh, useful. A bit clinging, but I think he rather liked that. Good Lord, you're not suggesting there was anything between them."

"Of course not."

"Oh, damn it," he expostulated. "A woman doesn't smother a man because he doesn't want to make love to her. I dare say she didn't either. I'll swear she didn't know the ropes."

"Naturally, I'm not suggesting anything of the sort. But you can't afford to overlook the most remote possibility, and if you take my view that your stepmother is innocent, then someone else is guilty."

"And you think it may be the Cobb? Ah, but you're a novelist. It's just the sort of thing you would suggest. You could do a fine thwarted woman psychological study out of it."

"And truth is even stranger than fiction," I reminded him dryly.

"She must be mad," he broke out after a minute. "Besides, I don't believe she could. . . . There's one thing, though. Irene wrote me once after the bust-up. I haven't got the letter now, but I remember it pretty well. She had somehow found out that Viola had let me have some money, and she wrote to say that by staying away I was making the situation impossible. But at least if I did mean to stay I needn't take his money. He was desperate, and he'd forbidden her to see me—Viola I mean. It was quite an hysterical letter. She must have known the effect it would have on me."

"Precisely. I wonder if she did have that key."

"She could have put it back in the house by now. Didn't she practically break in next morning? I remember Viola telling me."

"That would be part of the game. The innocent, eager secretary. . . . But how the devil will you prove anything?"

I quoted Crook's axiom about the rope.

"There's one other thing," he said, and he looked a bit white. "It's pretty beastly, but I suppose I'd better tell you. She suggested that—that Viola came here for other reasons than just to bring me money or see me. After all, I was her husband's son. She'd known me since I was a kid."

"She actually said that?"

"Yes."

"I wish you hadn't destroyed that letter," said I.

"Well, would you keep a letter like that?"

I had to admit that it was improbable.

"There's one thing I must ask you. Forgive the apparent impertinence. There never was any such feeling on your part?"

"Never." He spoke with the most intense earnestness. "She was a damned attractive woman, mind you, and could give points to most of the girls I meet, but she was my father's wife. I never thought of her as anything else. I was sorry for her, because he gave her a pretty poor run for her money—that much she admitted—and actually she told me she was going to leave him. She couldn't stand it any longer."

"She came to see you several times."

"Yes. I was a kind of refuge to her, the one person to whom she could talk. You can't discuss that kind of situation with strangers, and you can't always bottle it up. Then, too, she kept me in touch with new developments. She wanted to effect a reconciliation."

"Was your father willing?"

"Only on his own terms, and then, I think, only for a time. In any case, I wasn't."

"Not even to please Mrs. Ross?"

"Not even then."

"She had told you, you said, that she was proposing to leave him?"

"She said she couldn't stand it any longer. He was treating her like a moron, insulting her before the servants. I should say Marston's a hotbed of gossip about her."

"Did she speak of plans?"

"She said she could work. She was a woman with a good deal of force of character."

"I don't doubt it, but even for women of character jobs don't grow on every bush. You know, it was a bi hard on him in a way."

"It must have been rotten for her. Besides . . . " he hesitated.

"Well?"

"I don't want this broadcast unless it becomes essential, but my father was going to lose his job, and he knew it."

"Who says so?"

"Bellman. I went to see him when I was down there." Bellman was the headmaster of Teddy Ross's school.

"Did he say why?"

"Incompetence, I gather. Father has been warned more than once, but he was so obsessed by this wretched little textbook he was writing he really didn't pay any attention to his other work. And his boys were getting out of hand."

"That puts rather a different complexion on things."

"I don't see that it helps her much. Oh, Lord, if you could only make people believe she didn't do it. I can't tell you what it's been like for me all these weeks, knowing I could do nothing, nothing, to help."

I felt suspicion leap in my breast. That tone was more urgent than one would expect from a mere stepson. A fear that had barely existed before crystalized now. Was he telling me the truth when he said his feelings for her were those of a young man for his father's wife whom he admired? Was there more to it than that? Had Irene Cobb any grounds for her belief that the pair had been lovers? The thought was insufferable, but I could not drive it out.

"It's an ugly case," I muttered. "Our only hope to discover something fresh, some new line of argument, some unconsidered aspect of the circumstances, a novel explanation of some trifle the others have overlooked. And that's easier said than done. You knew her well, better, I suppose, than anyone else. . . . "

He eyed me askance. "I've often wondered whether I knew her at all." He was silent for a bit, then went on more quietly, "I cared for her a good deal, though not precisely in the way you suggested. She was a fascinating woman; she brought a feeling of adventure wherever she went. I tell you I don't believe she did it, but I believe she could have done it. And that's a thing you'd hesitate to say of a great many women, or men either for that matter. Not because they have conscientious scruples, but because they haven't got what Kipling calls the essential guts."

If he was her lover he was putting up a magnificent show. "If I'd thought of her in any other way, in any romantic light," he went on, "do you suppose I could have taken money from her? Of course not, though goodness knows, I needed it. She helped me several times. I didn't mind taking it; it came out of my father's pocket. You know, there were times when I believed she was actually afraid of what my father might do."

"Oh, come," I said, "she wasn't that sort of woman."

"It was alien to her temperament, but—how do we know what her life with him was like? She'd been married for eleven years, and I think she'd been pretty unhappy for at least half that time. It's that, more than anything he did to me, that makes me so antagonisitc to him."

"The prosecution would tell you he had cause. There's been a suggestion"—here I watched him closely —"that she came up to town to meet a lover."

73

He turned perfectly white, put out a hand and clutched the mantelpiece. "No," he said in low tones, "I don't believe that. I couldn't."

I didn't know what to think. "Your father had his suspicions," I said.

"I know. But it couldn't have been true, could it? She wouldn't have done that. I mean, I could understand her leaving him altogether, but not that. It makes a man look such a fool."

Though I still doubted his statement of their relations, it seemed as though circumstances were making us allies in the fight for Viola Ross's life; it was a queer thought that I was also in with Crook to try and push the responsibility onto this boy. I noticed how he had clenched his hands while he spoke—what muscular hands they were. And yet I didn't want to see him take her place in the dock. I'd have preferred some anonymous chap I shouldn't have to meet. But if this boy had been her lover, then all my pity for her would be killed. That was the one thing I couldn't endure to believe.

Young Ross turned to me. "I'm going to say a pretty foul thing, about as foul a thing as any man could say about his own father. Do you think there was a remotest chance he did it himself?"

"Suffocated himself?"

"It could be done?"

"I doubt it. And anyway, what's the motive?"

"He was losing his job; he may have realized he was losing his wife. She's not the sort of woman to live without a man, and once she'd left him, was independent of

74

him, she'd probably consider herself free to live her own life. There wasn't much left for him, and he was hideously jealous of her. That much we know, or he wouldn't suddenly have altered their domestic arrangements after five years. Well? Any takers?"

I considered. "The blood on the pillow?"

"He could have worked that."

"The clock in the hat box?"

"It's exactly the sort of thing he would think of."

"The stone out of the ring?"

"He might have had opportunity. He'd be the one man who would know about it."

"But—smothering himself? Damn it all man, it can't be done."

"I wonder. That would explain the inquiry agent, the fact that he'd sent for his lawyer. After all, once she was disinherited he had no hold over her."

"And he deliberately arranged to die the night before he changed his will?"

"Of course. That would provide motive."

He sounded plausible enough, but I couldn't accept such a theory. I haven't any considerable medical knowledge, but I couldn't believe that a man can smother himself and put the cushion with which the job is done back on the chair afterwards. No, it was ingenious but impossible.

Young Ross's hope died hard. He made a number of crazy suggestions, none of which would have held water for an instant in court.

"Then there must be some alternative explanation," he cried, "and we've got to find it. You know, we've been going round and round in circles, and every time we come back to the same place, and the answer is Viola."

It's an old gambit with novelists, the guilty man working desperately for the acquittal of the innocent party. Somehow, I'd always thought of it as exclusively fictional, not the kind of thing that could ever happen to one in real life.

"You know," young Ross was talking again, "it's maddening to think that if only things had happened just a little differently I might have been able to prevent all this."

"You?" I stared.

"Yes. I was down in that part of the world that night. That is, I was at Selby, the next station on the line. As near as a touch I went to see the old man. Then I reflected that as likely as not he'd refuse to see me. I should miss the last train back to town, and I had to be on duty early in the morning."

"What on earth were you doing down there?"

"You remember that robbery case they had at Selby quite recently? They hadn't been able to find a lot of the stuff—furs and so on."

"Didn't they think it had been shipped abroad?"

"That's the police explanation, of course. It's always the police explanation when they fall down on anything. But they've no proof. Now, it occurred to me that the stuff might have been hidden locally, and the thieves be possessing their souls in patience until the stink had died down. I know that part of the country very well. I explored all over the place when I was a kid, and I remembered a rather horrible thing that happened when I was about nine years old. A boy who was at school with me disappeared: people blamed the gypsies, and his mother thought he had been murdered. A small girl disappeared from the same neighborhood a week or two later, but her body was subsequently found. She had been murdered in a particularly ghastly fashion, and the general feeling was that the degenerate responsible for one death was probably responsible for the other. A year afterwards the body of the boy was found in a natural hiding place, a sort of cave. There had been a landslip and he had been prisoned like a rat in a trap. He was right under the earth so no one could hear him. It was an awful thing. The authorities put up a warning board—a second landslip had disclosed the entrance and as far as I know no other tragedy ever took place there. But it occurred to me that if the men were local they might know about the cave and they might have stored their booty there. I suppose it sounds a crazy idea to you, but in the newspaper world we're all out for scoops. Anything original, anything topical, anything, above all, that the other fellow doesn't know—and here might be an amazing chance. I grant you it was a one-hundred-to-one chance that the things wouldn't be there, but I was feeling pretty desperate, and I decided to take that chance. I went down to Selby and walked through the woods. When I got to the place I saw the old notice board had been taken down, or else someone had chucked it away for a lark. The place had a deserted look, as if people didn't go there much these days. I began to go along the sort of path that led to the cave, but I hadn't gone far before I saw the whole thing had been blocked up. There simply wasn't a hope of anything being hidden there. However, I was so bitten with the idea that I might go one better than the police that I hung about for some time thinking of other places—a disused quarry, an empty well, where the stuff might be, and I went poking my nose into places and, of course, learning nothing."

"You didn't go to your father's house at all?"

"No. I wish to Heaven I had. I might have been able to prevent all this. But by this time it had got pretty late and the train service at that hour of the night isn't very frequent—"

"You must have poked about quite a long time," I suggested.

"I suppose I did. I kept thinking of some new place to search—"

"And I dare say you met people whom you knew. It's practically your native town, isn't it?"

"Actually, I didn't meet a soul. I told you the place seemed deserted, and I wasn't in the town. Anyway, except for the holidays, I was hardly ever at Marston. It's a pretty dead place. Of course, the ones I knew at school aren't Marston men at all."

Very neat, I thought, and on the surface plausible enough. He hadn't met anyone at the station, and none of the officials had recognized him. It was only a small halt and the ticket collector was a boy of sixteen. No, there was no earthly reason why he should have been seen. But it was all very convenient for him.

"And you came up on the last train?"

"Yes. I stopped for a quick one at The Bird in Hand —and caught the 9.49. That got me back just before midnight."

"Not much doing on the local trains at night, I suppose."

"Just a few workingmen traveling between intermediate stations. There were more on the London train. It comes from the West."

"I expect you were a bit tired, glad of a night's rest. I know that sort of journey—all stops and no food."

"Oh, I was lucky. I managed to get some food. I was back pretty late, but fortunately, Mrs. Judges expects newspaper men to be erratic. I let myself in and I didn't see her till the next morning, when I came back from buying newspapers, and found her at the telephone. My stepmother had just rung off."

It had happened as all along I had felt it might. Inch by inch I had wormed my way into the fellow's confidence. I had become so genuinely interested that I had, for part of the time at all events, forgotten the end of my mission, which was to find someone—anyone—to put in Mrs. Ross's place. Young Ross had been so sincere in his telling of his story, that I had been swayed towards taking it at its face value. He had spoken with such candor, such genuine unhappiness about his stepmother's perils that, even against my own desires, I had begun to feel that it would be impossible to accuse this man of the crime. While he had all the time been covering the one tremendously important fact, namely, that he had been out all night.

He could not, of course, know that I had already heard Kenward's story. Perhaps he didn't even know that Kenward had seen him leaving the train. From the young engineer's manner I had not gathered that there was any degree of intimacy between the two. As for the landlady, Ross must have thought he had covered himself there; he had told her he had just been out and had flourished an armload of papers. I wondered, too, why he had brought all those papers in on that particular morning. It might, of course, have been to back up his story of having gone out early.

It followed, therefore, that he hadn't caught that train; probably he had come up on the first workman's train. That meant he had been in the neighborhood of Marston that night and hadn't left it until too late to catch the last train to town. His purpose for being there was a secret one or he would have spoken of it. That was the night his father had died: the son's motive, I argued, was equally as powerful as that of the wife: on the face of it, it seemed more like a man's than a woman's crime. Harry Ross had said he no longer had a latchkey to the front door. I wondered whether anything could be made of that.

"Look here," I said, "we'd better keep in touch with one another on this. Goodness knows where the real murderer is, what he's doing. If he suspects us he may try his hand at a second death. After all, you can't be hanged more than once. and if we work together, without being too obvious about it, at least one of us may always be on the spot. Besides, working in couples has several advantages."

He agreed at once. It had been perhaps a dangerous move on my part, but then the whole position was dangerous. I didn't want to risk a second murder, but there are some risks you have to take.

On my way down I encountered the landlady in the hall.

"I'm wondering whether you've got a room to let here," I said.

"For yourself?"

"Yes. I'm not in London a great deal, but I don't care about going to hotels all the time, and I expect to be up and down quite a bit during the next month or two. If you had something—I like a quiet house. . . . "

"You'll find this quiet enough. How soon would you be wanting it?"

"I'd like to take it at once, if you've got anywhere free."

"As it happens, I have, up at the top of the house."

"The top?"

"Well, that means you've no one overhead. That's something. It faces north, but then the summer's coming on, so it'll be nice and cool. And you'll be able to work up there if you want to. That Mr. Kenward's hardly ever in, and Mr. Ross mostly takes his meals out, though I can get them, if you give me notice."

"I expect I should be out a good deal," I said.

She took me upstairs to a big room with a sloping ceiling, and a tunnel to the window. It looked over rows and rows of roofs. This kind of view has always stimulated me. I like to feel myself in the heart of humanity, of movement, of passions and hopes. It was abominably furnished, but that didn't matter. It would be convenient to have some place where I could keep track of young Ross's visitors, follow up his movements.

Mrs. Judges stood in the center of the room, looking the picture of respectability, her arms folded, her face sharp and speculative. She told me the rent was fourteen shillings and cheap at that, because this was a respectable house, which was more than you could say for some of the neighbors. I closed with her at once, and put down two weeks' rent.

SIX

CROOK's appearance suits his name: he's a big, jocular, pot-bellied rascal, with the general air of a bookie on the course—not the gentlemanly Regent Street kind— with hands like hams and small, very bright gray eyes that never miss anything. If I'd been told he had been warned off the turf, or crossed off the register of solicitors for improper practice, I should have had no difficulty in believing this. He didn't look respectable, he wasn't a gentleman—indeed, he had no admiration for the species—and his clientele would have interested Scotland Yard. But he didn't know what it was to have a minute to spare, and he had a waiting list that far better known men might envy. He said to me once, "My office isn't a church; you won't find the Ten Commandments printed on the walls, but if you can pay for a job I'm your man. Innocence costs more than a lot of people would like to believe. Take my word for it, it costs a hell of a lot. But then it's worth a lot. If morality weren't damned expensive it wouldn't have any value at all. Show me any mug who wants it for its own sake."

"I've found out some things about your young man," he greeted me. "That is, Parsons has. He's been in pretty low water, y'know. I dare say Father's intention of altering his will hit him a bit hard. And there can't be much doubt that Ross was suspicious of his relations with Mrs. Ross. To be candid, Arnold, she does seem to have acted a bit crazily. After all, young Ross is a presentable chap—and if she was only takin' him money, as they both swear she was, why couldn't she have mailed it? Ross may have been a little tin god in that household but he couldn't interfere with His Majesty's Post Office. Or she could have sent the money in a registered envelope from London. The only thing she needn't have done was visit the fellow in his own rooms."

"And yet," I urged, "they don't seem to have made definite appointments. She once had to wait an hour for him."

Crook laid a pudgy finger against a nose that dominated the whole unscrupulous intelligent face. "The human heart is deceitful above all things and desperately wicked. See St. James. They say, don't they, that even the devil can cite scripture for his own purpose. Take it from me, there's no one can do it better. If she'd always found him in and ready for her, then Papa Ross might consider himself a wronged man. He seems to have had his doubts as it is."

"There's something wrong here anyway," I said. "That fellow of yours might turn his attention to discovering how Mr. Harry Ross spent the night of the fourth. His story is that he caught the last train back to the junction and got into town about midnight. But Kenward—who's a disinterested witness—swears he saw him leave the station at eight-thirty or thereabouts. I've consulted the time tables and that's just the time the first London train—the workman's train—arrives at Victoria."

"Your idea being that he visited his father—and polished him off?"

"He obviously visited someone—and doesn't want the details of the visit made public. If he wasn't with Ross, senior, where was he?"

"My strike, you're keen to see the fellow swung, aren't you?" suggested Crook.

"I'd rather he swung than Mrs. Ross did."

Crook looked at me, grinning malevolently. "Does the lady know of your interest in her?" he inquired.

I felt myself coloring furiously. "How should she? I'm simply a member of the jury to her, one more or less anonymous creature among a dozen. I've met her, but that's about all."

Crook shook his head. "Don't you believe it. That might have been true if she'd been a man. Women aren't like us. They ain't logical, Arnold, but they've got a quality that's often more useful than logic. You might call it instinct.

"A woman on trial for her life will assess each member of the jury as an individual in whose hands that life lies. She probably knows which of them are her implacable enemies by the time the trial's over. If Mrs. Ross were told that one man had saved her from a unanimous verdict of guilty, she could, I dare say, put her finger on that man. Don't for a moment imagine she thinks of you as a stranger. You've been connected with the most violent crisis that can happen to anyone. Women are intensely personal and if she met you on the street ten years hence she'd remember you—assuming, that is, that ten years hence she'll be in a position to recognize anyone in the street."

"I was wondering"—I felt I was speaking diffidently—"should I go and see her, or remain anonymous—or what?"

"If ever you have to handle women, Arnold, just remember their middle name is Vanity. That's true of the best of 'em. It's not their fault; the Almighty made 'em like that, and lucky for us he did. It gives us a handle in our dealings with 'em, and heaven knows we need it. They're like quicksilver, women are." He sunk his chin on his great fist. "Here one shape one minute and the other side of the board a totally different shape the next. Yes, it's lucky for us that they are anchored by vanity. It keeps 'em from running off the board altogether. By the way, do you?" He had a disconcerting habit, that I had noticed before, of returning to a remark or question at least two paragraphs old.

"Do I what?"

"Want to marry the lady."

"I happen to be engaged to someone else," said I.

"That does complicate matters. Well, well, there's a lot of complications here. First of all, it may interest you to know that your bird was in a very nasty net. Bookies. Not nice fellows, bookies, not when you're on the wrong side of them. And I don't fancy Papa Ross had much sympathy for chaps that dealt with them anyhow."

"So he'd got to get money," I exclaimed. "He didn't tell me that."

"You do expect to have your straw put into your hands, don't you?" he murmured. "Remember the devil's beatitude? Blessed is he that expecteth nothing. . . . Expecting things don't get you anywhere. You have to go out and fetch 'em."

"Then you think—"

"Tut, tut, man. I'm not paid to think. I've got to get the lady off, if it can be done. Thinking might be fatal."

I took Crook's advice and didn't go to see Viola Ross. In the circumstances I felt I couldn't conceivably suggest putting Harry Ross in her place. Better to get the whole case pat and then lay it before the proper authorities. I still couldn't get out of my mind a suspicion that she and the young man had been lovers, but possibly events would show. When I got back to Marston I went to look over the house. It was locked, and there was no one there, Martha having gone to work for some people in the neighborhood. I wondered whether she would help me at all; not willingly, I decided, for she had been on Teddy's side and would probably be glad to see his widow hanged. However, I took my chance, and having discovered her address, called at the house, going meekly to the side door. She was not a woman who worked well with others; girls had come and gone at The Laurels during the last five years, and now Martha had shown her wisdom by taking a post with an elderly woman who kept no other servants. I chose my time carefully. Waiting till the fussy old woman had been tucked up in rugs, despite the warmth of the afternoon, and driven off by a bored chauffeur, I rang the side bell. Martha herself opened the door. She recognized me, of course, but there was only hostility in her manner.

"I wonder if you could spare me ten minutes, Martha," said I.

Martha said something about the silver.

"I shan't stop you. You can go on cleaning the silver while I talk." I insinuated my way into the house. She didn't want to help me but, on the other hand, she didn't want to miss whatever my visit might portend. Grudgingly she told me to come in.

"If it's about Mrs. Ross I can't do anything to help," said she.

"Why should you think it's Mrs. Ross?"

"Why else should you be coming here?"

"That's logical enough. Yes, you're right. It is about Mrs. Ross."

"I can't tell you anything I didn't tell the court."

"You mean, you answered all the questions they put to you. That isn't quite the same thing."

"What does that mean?"

"I was on the jury, and I don't agree that the evidence proves a case against Mrs. Ross."

"Everybody else thought so."

"That's why I've come to see you now. I want to convince them."

"How do you think I can help you?" Her manner would have turned the milk rancid.

"You went to bed at ten o'clock, didn't you?"

"Yes."

"And you're a sound sleeper?"

"I need it. There's a mort of work in that house, and having to go round after that gel doing everything she's done over again."

"And Mrs. Ross went out soon after nine?"

"Well?"

"So that between ten and about half past eleven the house was virtually empty. I mean, if anyone had come in you wouldn't have heard them."

She admitted that with infinite reluctance. "Who do you suggest did come in?"

"I don't know yet. But you admit it was possible that someone could."

"How would he get in? The back door was locked and bolted. I see to it myself every night as soon as the girl's gone."

"You're afraid of tramps?"

"If I am I've got good reason. Did you never hear of that case in Manchester where the servant was found on the kitchen floor with her throat cut, and they never found the man that did it?"

"You think that might happen here?"

"Seeing what has happened here," said she significantly, "it isn't so surprising."

"Anyway, you're sure you locked the back door that night?"

"Take my Bible oath on it."

"And the front door?"

"That has a Yale lock. You couldn't break through that."

"Is there any other way of getting in? What about the windows?"

"They were all bolted. I saw to that myself. All on the ground floor, that is. Unless this man you're thinking about was a human fly, he couldn't walk up a wall."

"There's no other way in?"

"There's the garden door, of course, but—"

"Where's that?"

"It leads out of the end of the hall into the garden."

I sat up, rigid with excitement. "The garden slopes down to Little David Lane, doesn't it? All the houses in the terrace have gardens opening on that lane. And there's a door in the wall for each house. So that anyone could turn out of Romary Street into the lane and push open the green wooden door—would that be kept locked, too?"

"Never seen a key to that door. The gate was never used, anyway. All Mr. Ross's friends and hers came to the front, and mine and the tradesmen came to the side."

"Suppose someone came up through the garden—"

"Knowing the house was going to be empty? You're supposing a lot."

"He may not have known. He may have come to see Mr. Ross, and then, finding the house dark—what about a light in the hall?"

"I put that out when I went to bed. Mr. Ross had expense enough without throwing money away."

"Suppose he rang the bell, no one would hear?"

"No one."

"And if it was someone who knew the house, he might go around to the back and see if there was a light in any of those windows?"

"He might."

"In which case, he would come through the garden?"

"That's right."

"Could he conceivably get in through the garden door—into the house, I mean?"

The old woman hesitated.

"He could?" I pressed the question.

"Not unless he knew the house, he couldn't."

"What do you mean?"

"There's something a bit wrong with that lock, has been for ages. The key turns, but not all the way."

"So the door could be opened from the outside."

"Only if you thumped at it. Most people would think it was locked."

"But someone who knew the house from the inside would know?"

"Yes, I suppose he would."

"And once he was in and knew the lie of the house, he might go upstairs looking for someone?"

"He'd have a nerve."

"It takes nerve to kill a man."

"Why should he go to Mr. Ross's room?"

"Perhaps he was looking for Mr. Ross."

"Then why didn't he go to the right room? It was only when he was laying down for a bit of sleep like

this that Mr. Ross slept in that room. It used to be
Mr. Harry's. . . ."

I just suppressed an exclamation.

"Isn't it more likely," I said, "that he thought the
house was empty and probably had a most fearful shock
when he found someone in that bed? And if he happened to see Mr. Ross beginning to wake it might be
instinctive to put the pillow over his head to prevent
his giving the alarm?"

"Yes, I suppose it could have happened like that.
But how are you going to show it did?"

"I don't know—yet."

Neither did I, but I felt I had made a definite ad-
vance. That afternoon I went around to the house by
way of Little David Lane. The door in the wall opened
easily and I walked up the garden. I dare say no one
had walked up there for weeks. There was a little
summerhouse halfway up the path, and I went in there
to meditate. It was the usual affair, like an enlarged
dovecote, with a wooden seat. I sat down and pulled
out my cigarette case. I had just pitched the match
away when suddenly I stooped and picked up something lying at my feet. It was the stub of a half smoked
cigarette. It may have lain there for ages; the summerhouse was dry enough. I looked at it carefully. It
was marked X.X.X. I sat back, my heart pumping.
I recalled Harry Ross saying, "Have a cigarette? They're
only gaspers. My father says no one but a kaffir could
smoke them, but they're cheap. I get them from a
chap in Houndsditch." They had been rank enough
to make me choke. I had never smoked anything so

strong. And here, on the floor of the summerhouse, was a stub of a cigarette of that unusual make. I went around carefully, almost on hands and knees. I didn't find another cigarette, but I found the stub of a wax vesta. I sat there for a long time with my two discoveries lying on the palm of my hand.

At first sight it seemed as though I had achieved something, but except to myself these clues would not bring much conviction. It is always difficult to persuade English people of a case of parricide. They are far more ready to believe in guilty wives. Wives often can't escape their bonds except by death, but young men have a number of other outlets. They can walk away, contrive a living by hook or crook, they haven't taken vows, owe no duty—not at least as many a wife thinks that she owes it— What I had was young Ross's story, that I could prove to be false, his own acknowledgment that he had been in the neighborhood that night, his very lame story to account for his presence there— None of that would cut very much ice with a jury. Nevertheless, I had to prove to that jury's satisfaction that he had actually been in the house, and I didn't know how I should do it.

Crook's people worked fast. Within forty-eight hours he had news for me.

"Your friend, Harry Ross, likes his fun," he informed me. "And I should say that he was in about as awkward a jam as anyone need want. I told you there was a bookie—a nasty bookie at that. The suave Regent Street kind that goes to court, when he realizes that

Papa has the necessary. And if Papa had refused to pay up it might have been mighty unpleasant for the son. He'd apparently pledged Father's credit, and he had to get hold of the money if he didn't want to get into very nasty trouble indeed."

"And he came down to see Ross that night—I don't suppose he did see him to talk to—but he came to the house. . . ."

"You're sure of that?"

I produced the cigarette and match. Crook whistled softly. "That was neat. When was he officially there last?"

"Best part of a year. This must be fairly recent."

"And no one else in the place smokes them?"

"No one. I should say no one used that garden much. It has an air of dereliction."

Crook scoffed. "Oh, you novelists! Why can't you say it's a wilderness? Dereliction my foot."

"Anyhow," said I, rather nettled, "there you are." I told him about my interview with Martha. "You might put your fellow on to finding out where Harry Ross really was that night."

"Thanks," said Crook curtly. "When I want to be shown my job I'll apply to you. You seem pretty sure. Do you imagine Mrs. Ross knew about this?"

"I'm sure she didn't." I heard the vehemence in my voice and was a little surprised.

"How can you be sure?"

"How could she know?"

"She might have come in while he was in the house."

94

"She wouldn't have stood her trial and not said a word."

"Mightn't have been much use her saying a word. Who was going to believe it wasn't a put-up job?"

I sat back, thinking. "Suppose she's found guilty at the next trial?"

"It's like the old fairy tale. Why should two die where one will suffice? There'll be plenty of people prepared to believe that the pair were lovers. People like their romance highly seasoned, you know."

"She didn't get back till nearly half past eleven. If we could show that by that time he was somewhere else. . . ."

"I'm only warning you, you may not be able to have everything. All right, you'd better leave the next move to us. We'll keep in touch."

"Remember, Mrs. Ross's life depends on this," said I.

"And my reputation is involved. Don't forget that, Arnold. A poor thing, no doubt, a poor thing but mine own."

I came away from his office feeling seriously perturbed. I knew it wouldn't be possible to prove that that cigarette-end had been left in the summerhouse on the day of Ross's death, but the fellow might find it difficult to explain how it had got there. And—the same question maddened me. Had there been anything between them? Should I ever know? I told Crook I had acquired a London address; when he heard where it was he groaned.

"Why? In heaven's name, why? Ever heard of *Through the Looking-Glass*? Yes. Then you'll remember that the immortal prig who was the heroine of that story only reached her objective by walking away from it. That's how the best detective work is done. Once you let this fellow see that you suspect him, it's like a burglar breaking into a room, complete with face-mask and jemmy, and making for the lady wearing the handsomest pearls. What you want to do is to get into a boiled shirt and look so like a gentleman that nobody spots the difference."

"Is there really any difference?" I asked.

Crook grinned. "Well, they don't actually teach any of the useful arts at Eton or Harrow yet, but it's amazing how their boys pick up tips all the same. You should ask Bill."

"I don't think I've put young Ross on his guard," I protested. "I've enlisted him as an ally."

"And if he's got the mind of a louse he'll ask himself why—game *and* rubber, what?" He grinned, and I stood up to go.

SEVEN

It was three days later that the anonymous letters began.

First of all I received a telephone call from Bunty. In deference to her father's feelings, I wasn't making myself in any way conspicuous with her, so long as I was involved in the Ross affair. I knew the kind of girl she was; as true as a rock, as honest as daylight. I didn't even grudge her going about with Denis Markham and any other young man who wanted to squire her. A girl like that is bound to be popular, and it wasn't as if, in the circumstances, I could take her about a lot myself, as I've said. I had been up to London to see my publisher, and when I got back I found a message from Bunty. "Come and see me tonight, if you can," it said.

I went, of course. I was relieved to hear that the colonel was out. Mrs. Friar was never much in evidence; in any case she was a quite negligible woman, interested mainly in philanthropic activities. I never knew how she came to have a daughter like Bunty. Bunty herself looked lovely but troubled.

"Richard, darling, would you do something for me?"

"Practically speaking, anything."

"Is that a promise?"

"You must tell me what I'm promising."

She hesitated. "I want you to give up this case," she said at last.

I stared at her in amazement. "Bunty! You don't know what you're saying."

"It's you that don't know—don't know your own danger."

"What do you mean by danger? Do you think I'm going to fall in love with her?"

"No, no. I never thought of that. You told me—you told me—"

"There's no one on earth I want to marry but you," said I. "So where's the danger?"

"This." She had been holding one hand behind her back all the time we were talking, and now she withdrew it and let me see a letter clasped between her fingers.

"Who's that from?"

"I don't know. It's that kind of letter."

"That kind's better put on the fire," said I austerely.

"It may mean what it says."

"What does it say?"

"You'd better read it."

I took it from her. It was a sheet of plain, fairly cheap paper, of the kind found in typewriting offices; there was no signature, just the two lines of typewriting.

If your friend is wise he will drop the Ross affair. Tell him this.

Melodrama could scarcely go further.

"You're not taking this seriously," I urged.

"Of course I am. Do be sensible, Richard. Don't you see whoever sent that is probably the murderer, and a man who's killed one person won't stop at killing another."

I was onto that like a flash. "Then you admit that Mrs. Ross didn't kill her husband?"

"I don't know. . . ."

"You said this person—the writer of this letter—is probably the murderer."

"Why else should he write it?"

"Precisely. It means that he or she is afraid of my finding something out. Don't you see, darling, I can't stop now?"

"But if I ask you?"

"How can I? There's a woman's life at stake."

"There's your life at stake. That matters more to me."

"Bless you for that, but if I threw this up out of sheer funk—it would be that—and they hanged Mrs. Ross, we'd never know a moment's peace."

"I should forget her."

"You might. But I shouldn't. Don't make things too difficult for me, my darling. After all, if I were a soldier, we might have to be separated, to take risks. This is simply a job I must do. I didn't get myself put on the jury, but since I was there I can't evade my responsibilities."

"And what about this?" She tapped the letter.

"I'm afraid that's a chance I have to take. If I was resolved before, I'm doubly resolved now."

"So even for me—"

"Darling, I've explained to you, I can't."

Twenty-four hours later the second anonymous letter arrived. This time it was for me, bore the local postmark and said, "Remember that discretion is the better part of valor and get out while you can." The paper was the same as that used for the first message, and so was the type.

I took it around to Bunty. "I wonder how many machines there are in this town," said she.

"Numbers, I should think. Of course, the fact that it has a local postmark may simply be a blind. It may not have been written in Marston at all."

"I suppose not. All the same. . . ." I could see her mind working behind her clear eyes, but she refused to say another word. "I only want to help you, Richard, not confuse you."

"Promise me you won't butt in on this," I begged her. "That I couldn't stand."

"I'm in already," said she serenely.

"What do you mean?"

"You can't be in anything and leave me behind."

Well, what can you do with a girl like that!

Our correspondent, however, had not finished with us. At the end of the week the third letter arrived. This came to Bunty again.

Tell your friend he has twenty-four hours left in which to change his mind.

Bunty was in a frantic state. "Don't you see, Richard, whoever it is will stop at nothing. You've got to give it up. It won't help Mrs. Ross for you to be dead, too."

"Don't *you* see," I urged, "it's all bluff? Got to give it up indeed! And suppose I did decide not to go on, darling, how would our friend know? Believe me, darling, it's sheer bluff. Nothing more."

"But why?"

"Because I'm dangerous. Because I may be on the track of the truth. That's why."

"It won't be any comfort to me your being on the right track when you're in the cemetery," retorted Bunty with spirit.

"I can't give it up now," I said. "You must see that."

"Then will you spend the next twenty-four hours here, with me?"

"And risk someone putting a bullet in your brain, too? No, darling, I won't."

"You must think a lot of this Mrs. Ross," remarked Bunty, with the first sign of suspicion she had shown.

"I shouldn't think of myself, and I don't see how you could think much of me if I dropped it now, against my most powerful convictions, simply because it was a bit dangerous."

I didn't alter any of my arrangements for that twenty-four hours. I decided that next day I would go up and see Crook and get his advice. I didn't suppose he would mind in the least if I were shot; he would say it was my own fault for not being able to keep out of the limelight. His only concern would be for his fees.

During that day I was out a good deal; no one

threatened my security, although I brushed shoulders with innumerable people. I found that I was keeping largely to public places, I didn't go down short cuts, or linger in lonely by-ways. Bunty was having lunch with me and afterward I was taking her into X— to the pictures. It was not precisely a successful afternoon. Bunty paid no attention to what I was saying or to the film. She was convinced that my enemy was at my side, that at any instant the tragedy would occur.

"This isn't a gangster film," I told her once rather irritably. "This is twentieth century England."

"And very odd things are happening in it," retorted she, refusing to be reassured. I took her to tea at the famous Grey Goose, where Charles II is reported to have hidden when he was in flight. There is a magnificent oaken staircase and a door several inches thick, with a bolt heavy enough to brain a man; and at the top of the house they show you a kind of cupboard that is supposed to be haunted. Apparently a mysterious child who would have been England's heir—so the legend runs—was concealed there, and its guardian was slain before news of the infant's hiding place could be received, and long afterward a tiny skeleton was discovered mouldering behind the door. It was a gruesome story, and seemed to add to the gloom of the day. Bunty was obsessed by the notion that danger lurked for me in that closet, and refused to come upstairs and look at it.

"No one knew I was going to bring you here," I urged, but she would not be shaken.

"I wish you weren't going to London tomorrow,"

she said. "I wish I needn't let you out of my sight. I wish the police wouldn't arrest people for murder unless they've got clear proof they're guilty. I wish you hadn't got a legal novelist's mind. I wish we were married and the other side of the world."

I echoed the last wish heartily enough.

It was late when I deposited Bunty at her own home, with the promise that I would ring her up later in the evening and assure her of my own well-being. Derek Markham was there, pottering the garden with the colonel. They both came to the gate.

"Thought you were never coming back," growled the colonel.

"We've had a wonderful day," said Bunty.

"You're looking tired."

"I feel radiant. How are you, Derek?"

Derek looked rather washed out. I wasn't surprised. I heard he had been there for over an hour, and an hour of Colonel Friar's conversation would weary the most powerful physique.

"Thought you might come out with me tonight," he said to Bunty, looking at me with a scowl.

"Not tonight," said Bunty quickly. "I have to be in tonight."

She avoided looking at me.

"Why don't you go?" I said, but she shook her head.

"Another night, Derek. Good-bye, Richard. You'll let me know about—you know what."

Colonel Friar was furious—furious with me for having kept his daughter out so long, furious with her for having refused to go out with young Markham. I felt suddenly exhausted, as if I were trying to hunt my way out of a thicket, with the thorns tripping me up on every side. I wished desperately that the whole thing were over, Viola Ross free, and myself safely married to Bunty. I was beginning to be afraid, and I knew that that was fatal.

I let myself in, with my thoughts full of the future. I have a little flat on the ground floor, whose sitting room windows look over a stony piece of garden, thickly sown, like all similar plots of ground, with laurel bushes. As I opened the door I paused a moment on the threshold; it seemed to me that the room was very cold. The day had been warm enough early, but during the afternoon a sharp wind had sprung up; it seemed to me now as though it swept in and filled the room. I put out my hand to turn on the electric light, but when I pressed the switch nothing happened. The bulb here was new, so that it should have flashed instantly into brilliance, in place of which I remained standing in the dark. I put my hand into my pocket and drew out a box of matches. Striking one, I lifted it above my head and took a step into the room. There was a flash, an explosion; I leaped backward. The match went out; I fumbled for a second. By the time it was lighted the room was perfectly quiet again. I felt that the sound of the explosion should have aroused everyone in the flats, but no one stirred. I remained in the darkened room for another minute, but still nothing happened. Then I went back to the hall, detached the light from its socket and came back to my sitting room. When I felt for the switch it was easy to understand why nothing had happened when I pressed the button. The bulb had been taken clean out. I fitted in the one in my hand and switched the current on. I saw why I had felt so cold as I came in. The french window that I had left latched but slightly ajar—you know those contraptions that enable you to ventilate your room without being completely blown away—now swung wide open. At my feet on the carpet lay a strand of thick black twine, the thing over which I must have stumbled as I came in. This led to the window. It's an old trick, though not one that is much resorted to in these days. You fix your weapon in some convenient spot, attach a string to the trigger, put the other end of the string in some place where a newcomer is bound to fall over it, and hare for the other end of the country. X comes in, falls over your booby-trap, the gun explodes, and he's done for. All the same, such a method has its dangers.

"This," I told myself grimly, "is a matter for the police."

I got Fisher on the telephone. "Who is it?" he said.

"My name is Arnold."

"Arnold who?"

"Richard Arnold."

"Have you lost a sealyham terrier?"

"No, I have not. I've never had a sealyham terrier. I don't like sealyhams. If I had a dog it wouldn't be a sealyham."

I heard a voice, off, saying, "No, it's not the dog." And then, "What is it?"

"An attempt at murder, I think," said I.

"Domestic fracas," said the voice off again.

"Nothing of the kind," I yelled. "Some chap's tried to murder me in my own house."

"Better come down to the station and report," advised Fisher's prim voice. I don't believe the Last Day will disturb that inhuman calm of the police. Like doctors, they're unshockable—until someone turns the guns on them.

"I think it would be better if you came up here," said I. "You'll want to examine the scene, won't you?"

"Is anyone killed?"

"No thanks to X, whoever he may be, if I'm not."

"What happened, sir?"

"Only the trick of the tethered gun."

"Ah! What happened?"

"You'd better come and see," I responded irritably, and hung up the receiver.

Without undue haste, and with no appearance of apprehension, Fisher came up to my house. He listened gravely to what I had to say and stooped his head to look at the length of twine that was still attached to a shrub beyond the window.

"Any idea why anyone should want to murder you, sir?" he inquired. It crossed my mind that he would have made a marvelous butler. He had a suavity that seemed unnatural off the stage, where to me everything always seems a shade over life-size.

"To prevent being officially murdered himself," said I.

Fisher's face wore a half pained, half shocked expression. The perfect butler all over again when the youthful heir gets into a mess.

"Meaning?"

"That X, whoever he may be, is aware of my activities in the Ross case."

Fisher's lips turned down. "You're still following that up?" He didn't say sir this time.

"My convictions haven't undergone any change," I agreed.

Fisher shrugged; he seemed to regard me as the Church of the Middle Ages regarded the man who went out of the congregation of the faithful in an attempt to establish his own beliefs. The Inquisition would have burned him in state at the next auto da fe. Fisher seemed to intimate that since I chose to disagree with the police it was illogical in me to expect their protection.

"Anyhow, here are the facts. I returned to find the bulb removed from my light, my window open, and a gun neatly rigged up."

"Have you got the gun, sir?"

"I haven't. Whoever had it seems to have waited to see what luck his plan had, and then vamoosed."

"Taking the gun with him?"

"He had time. I had to pull myself together, get a light, cross the room."

Fisher walked across to the window. "H'm. Thread's been snapped here. No," he stooped lower. "It's been cut. With scissors, I should say. That's a bit unusual. You'd expect them to use a knife."

"I'd have expected him to wind up the thread and take the whole thing with him," said I. "Men have been betrayed by less than a thread before now. What about Robinson and the bloodstained match?"

Fisher wasn't at all impressed. He was stooping over the branch. "See here, it got caught round a twig. That's why X cut it—the thread, I mean. I suppose he waited to take the gun in case it was traced to him. You say the bullet didn't touch you?"

"No, it went into the wall. You'll have to dig it out. The landlord won't be any too pleased. Well, well, so the fellow did mean what he said."

Fisher whipped around. He showed his first sign of excitement. "What does that mean?"

"He told me if I didn't quit these twenty-four hours would be my last."

"He *told* you that?"

"Yes."

"Who told you?"

"Presumably the fellow who rigged up this little booby-trap."

"But who is he?"

"That I can't tell you. He didn't sign his name."

"Oh! You mean anonymous letters."

"That's right."

"Sent to you?"

"One to me and two to Miss Friar."

"Miss Friar, eh?" He whistled softly. "Why her?"

"I suppose the writer thought she might exercise some authority over me."

"Like that, is it? Well, it didn't make much difference."

"Did you suppose it would?"

"Did he tell you he was going to shoot you today?"

"He told me if I didn't lay off I should be giving the undertaker a job."

"And you didn't?"

"I didn't do anything today beyond telephoning my man in town, and how the devil he knew about that—"

"Perhaps he wasn't taking any chances anyhow."

"It seems not."

"Have you got the letters here?"

"Yes. In my drawer."

"I'd like to see them. Did you think to keep the envelopes?"

"Aren't I a novelist?" I grinned. "Kept the whole caboodle."

I crossed the room and pulled open a drawer. I knew exactly where I had put them. They weren't there any longer. I looked, as a matter of form, through all the other drawers, but I knew I shouldn't find them in any of them. And I didn't. They had utterly and completely disappeared.

"He's got a cool head," was Fisher's dry comment.

"He wasn't taking much risk," I pointed out. These apartments had been constructed out of a block of old houses, and lacked a good many of the advantages of the modern mansions. But they had compensations. They had large rooms, air, were soundly built, you didn't hear every movement of the fellow overhead as if he were on the other side of a lath partition; and they had what the new flats never achieve, a sense of space and time. Old-fashioned furniture suited them, they were solid and restful. I've tried often to work in modern flats and hotels, but never with any success; hurry seems to be in the very atmosphere. These five houses, that had been thrown into the block of flats known as Clarence House, all had little gardens at the back. The wall around these was not very high; a man could easily scale it, and as they backed onto some waste ground he could come and go unseen. He might even leave the flats by the front entrance; no one would be likely to notice him if he did. There were several new tenants who would not recognize one another.

"Do you want to look around?"

"Routine." Fisher relaxed sufficiently to grin. "But you've been over the place yourself. He's not likely to have left many traces."

When he had examined the room he went into the garden, but the drought of the past fortnight had made any hope of footprints out of the question. He found a policeman patrolling the side of the street, and asked him if he had seen a man come over the wall, but the man said he hadn't.

"I bet he lay pretty low," Fisher agreed. "Besides, he needn't have come over the wall here. He could have run along at the foot and climbed over onto that patch of building land."

As a matter of principle he made an examination, but neither of us expected to find much.

"Is it necessary to broadcast this?" I asked.

"When we consider it necessary we shall take steps," said Fisher.

EIGHT

After Fisher had gone an idea occurred to me. I lifted the telephone and called the number of Mrs. Judges' house. When I got a reply I asked for Harry Ross. A voice said, "I don't think he's in. He told me he wouldn't be wanting dinner."

"Could you find out?" I asked. "It's rather important."

I waited for what seemed ages. Then the woman came back. "He isn't in his room. He hasn't been back all day. He said he'd be late, about eleven, he told me."

I looked up the railway guide. Supposing that Harry Ross had been the man waiting by the laurel bushes when I arrived and that he had hurried off immediately, he could have caught a train that would get him back to London about 9.30. I took down the receiver again, and telephoned the station. I knew the station master, and asked for him personally.

"Hullo," said I. "Mr. Arnold speaking. I understood from Mr. Harry Ross that he was coming down today, but he hasn't arrived. Have you heard anything of him?"

Marston is small enough for the comings and goings of its regular citizens to be noticed. Babbage said he'd heard nothing. He'd ask if I liked. He did ask, but without result. No one had seen a trace of young Ross.

I decided to go to town next day and see Arthur Crook. Before I started, the telephone rang.

"Richard." It was Bunty's voice. "They did try and get you last night."

"They didn't succeed."

"They may next time."

"You think there'll be a next time?"

"Of course. You're a dangerous person. Oh Richard, can't you give it up?"

"Because I'm frightened? Bunty, you don't mean that."

"I do. There's nothing Old School Tie about me. I don't want you handed to me in a coffin."

"I don't want any of us to end prematurely in a coffin," said I soberly. "Besides, the fellow, whoever he is, is obviously a killer. I couldn't drop the thing now. The police are on to it. Fisher's making inquiries."

"Has he any ideas?"

"The police don't confide in us, darling, but I'll tell you one thing he thinks."

"What's that?"

"That I deserve all that's coming to me for daring to doubt the police."

"I don't feel you're safe out of my sight," wailed Bunty.

"I shall be safe enough today. I'm going to London."

"London's worse than Marston. People are always getting accidentally killed in London."

"It isn't accidents we need be afraid of," said I, gravely.

"That's what I mean. Can't I come with you?"

"No. Definitely not."

"Promise you'll ring me up tonight."

"I can't do that. I might be prevented."

"What do you mean?"

"I don't know where I shall be tonight, whom I shall be with. It might be impossible, and then you'd start imagining horrors."

"I shall imagine those anyhow."

"What are you going to do today?"

"Derek wants me to go out with him."

"You'd better go," I said. "It'll take your mind off me."

"You will ring me up if you can."

"If you'll realize that if I don't it doesn't mean I'm stretched in a mortuary."

I rang off. It was an unsatisfactory position, and the sooner the affair was settled the better I should be pleased.

I got in touch with Fisher before I left, but he had nothing to tell me.

"We're the police here," said he reprovingly, "not greased lightning."

Up in London I went straight to Crook's office. "I told you to keep out of this," said Crook unsympathetically. "You're making my job twice as hard, and then you'll probably boggle at my fees. If I had my way that text—'The laborer is worthy of his hire'—would be hung over every breakfast table."

"On the contrary, I'm providing you with evidence," I retorted.

"How do you make that out?"

"Didn't you tell me that if you gave a man sufficient rope, he always ended by hanging himself?"

"Now look here," said Crook. "I'll provide all the necessary rope. Get that."

"And every scrap of evidence," I went on undaunted, "that I can show you . . . "

"That's just what you aren't doing. You haven't got anything to show me. What's the use of your having anonymous letters if you let them be poached before they reach me?"

"When this fellow realizes he hasn't shot his bolt he may write another."

"Why should he? He's given you warning and to spare."

"You might think it worth your while to find out how Master Ross was amusing himself last night," I suggested. "He wasn't at home."

"Oh, you know that, do you? Do you know where he was officially?"

"I could find out. I dare say he'll have a perfectly good alibi that can be proved six times over."

"The perfectly good ones are the ones that can't be proved at all. They can't be disproved either."

I was resolved to put an end to this difficult situation as soon as I could. I knew this was just one of a number of cases to Crook, but it had turned into a life or death affair for me. I went along to Vane Street, wondering whether I should find Ross in. He wasn't, but Kenward was. He had been doing a nightshift at the garage, and was having a meal when I arrived. A little later he tapped on my door.

"I heard you come up," he said, "and I wondered if you had a fill of tobacco. I must have a pipe, and I've run myself clean out. I could go out, of course, but it's begun to rain."

I offered him my pouch. "Ross isn't away, is he?" I asked.

"He's sleeping here, but that's about all he is doing."

"Ah, I wondered. I tried to get him last night."

"He was going to the dog races, or so he told me. It's a mug's game, betting."

"I suppose if you have an inside knowledge of form . . . "

"Even then there's a strong element of chance. And Ross doesn't know. He goes down every single time."

"I wonder he goes. Betting wasn't in Teddy Ross's line. He played for safety all along."

"And look where it landed him. Any further developments there, by the way?"

"We're no nearer a solution."

"Still have to give the police best."

"Not exactly. There's dirty work at the crossroads. Precisely how dirty we aren't sure yet. I suppose you don't know whether Ross has been—threatened?"

"Couldn't say. So far as I know, not at all. But then he isn't exactly poking his nose into it as you are."

"I wish he'd come in," said I.

"He's got a bit of a job at the moment. Addressing envelopes for an election. As soon as this affair's over he talks of going abroad. Much the best place for him. There isn't room in England for a man like that, and the colonies want men with a bit of capital. Besides, it's a much better life than hanging about in an office, rushing off after every piddling little bit of scandal that turns up."

"Did he lose on the dogs last night?" I wondered aloud.

"I haven't seen him since he came in. I was off about nine. I knew there'd been a call for him because Mrs. Judges came to my room to ask if I'd seen him."

"I'd be happier to see him in the flesh," I observed. "There's too much underground work about this job for me."

"It'll be a good thing, too, for him. He's getting jumpy. I fancy he thinks a good deal of that stepmother of his and there's no doubt he's got a guilty feeling."

"But it wasn't anything to do with him," I exclaimed.

"Not directly. But if she hadn't been helping him things mightn't have been so difficult at home, and Ross might still be alive. That's what he feels."

"Is that what he says?"

"He has said so."

You see the implications of that? It meant that Ross either believed his stepmother to be guilty or wanted to give the impression that he did.

"He talked of putting a bullet through his head the other day. He's a neurotic type."

"Has he got a gun?"

"I don't suppose so. It was just a figure of speech. Anyway, the fellow that talks about making a hole in the water never does."

After Kenward had gone down again I resolved to take a chance. Ross's room was on the floor below mine; I didn't suppose it would be locked, and I hoped he might not be back for lunch. I met Mrs. Judges on the stairs, and she said that he usually was out all day. She didn't know whether it was worth my while to wait. I said I'd stop in a little longer, and when I heard her go down to the basement I went into Ross's room. There was very little furniture in it—a chest of drawers, a bed, a table, a couple of chairs. On the table stood a typewriter with a soft cover over it. I stopped dead in my tracks. Of course, Ross would have a typewriter. Wasn't he a budding journalist? But could I prove to official satisfaction that this was the machine upon which the letters had been typed? True, the original letters were no longer available, but there might be others. I took up a slip of paper, pulled the soft cover off the machine, and typed a couple of lines. I was afraid to stay long. Heaven only knew what excuse I could give if I were found here.

"Now is the time for all good men to come to the aid of the party," I wrote.

Then I crumpled the paper in my hand, covered the machine again, and listened intently. There was no sound to be heard but a faint clashing of plates in the basement. I didn't stay more than a minute. I found no trace of a revolver, but then I hadn't expected to. If I had been asked to hazard a guess I should have said

117

that it lay in the mud and weeds of the river that runs through Lower Marston. Even dragging would be unlikely to reveal it, so deep and swift does the river run at certain points.

That night I did catch Ross at home. "I wanted to ask you something," I said.

"Well?"

"It's just this. Have you been favored with anonymous communications about this affair?"

"Good God, no. Why? Have you?"

"Yes. I'm putting the matter in the hands of the police."

"The devil you are. I didn't know you were so friendly with the police as all that."

"I pay my taxes, don't I? And they help to keep the police force going. When my life's being threatened I don't see why they shouldn't do their stuff on my behalf, whether I'm popular with them at the moment or not. After all, my life is more valuable even than my pride."

"Your life?" He lifted to mine a face from which every vestige of color had gone.

"It's come to that."

"In your shoes I'd begin to be scared."

"I was scared a long time ago. It's like everything else. You get accustomed to it."

"Aren't you nervous of going about alone?"

"I might be more nervous of going out *a deux*. You never know when a sideboard will conceal a hamadryad. However, to show there's no ill-feeling, come to the pictures tonight."

"I'd like to," said Ross, "but I don't care for the pictures. Why don't you come to the dog races with me?"

"Do you go regularly?"

"Pretty well. The poor man's race course."

I was standing by the window that was open, and I leaned forward to get a glimpse of someone passing below. I thought it was Bill Parsons, but I couldn't be sure. As I shoved my head through the window I felt a hand on my waist; an instant later the grip tightened. I struggled.

"You silly ass!" I said, pushing backwards. Ross gave a jerk, and I was safe in the room again.

"What the devil . . . ?" I began.

He was as white as I. "I thought you were going out on your head," he exclaimed.

"So did I for a minute."

"Those windows are so jolly near the ground. They're really rather dangerous."

"They are," I agreed. There was a minute's silence, then I said, "Thanks very much for your invitation. I'd like to come to the races. Have a meal with me first, won't you?" So we settled that.

I knew, of course, that I was playing with fire, but there are times when that kind of thing can't be avoided. No one was more anxious than I to see the end of the affair, but there are occasions in life, of which this was one, when it's more difficult to draw back than to go on. I imagined myself telling my story to Arthur Crook. I couldn't swear that Ross had tried to shove me out of the window; my foot had slipped an inch or two. He had only to say that he was trying to save me and that would be the end.

I spent the afternoon in a movie, and then went on to the Berkeley for a drink. I was meeting Ross at seven-thirty and we were going down to Wood Lane together. I kept a careful eye on him on platforms and mounting and alighting from omnibuses. He seemed quite unconcerned, produced a card, and told me the dogs he proposed to back, and appeared to have put all thought of this morning's misadventure out of his head. I was lucky in my backing; lucky is the word. I knew nothing about the dogs, and I just plunged. Ross was very scientific and unfortunate; I insisted on taking him to a bar afterwards and standing him beer and sandwiches. We parted on the stairs at Mrs. Judges'; he asked me in for a final whisky and soda, but I was playing for safety. I locked the door of my room, and didn't go to bed for a long time. I sat up, writing to Bunty, whom, after all, I hadn't telephoned. I hoped when she got my letter she'd forgive me.

I tried to be reassuring; actually, there was very little to tell. After I had stamped my letter I slipped out and put it in the post. It had missed the midnight mail, but it would catch one in the early morning, and at least it would bear today's date. I came back through a silvered street, thinking deeply of the past and the future, of Viola Ross and of Bunty, of the difference in the two women, of my new novel and the one I should write when this was done. I didn't hurry. I tested the mattress thoughtfully; I'd known worse, and in any case I wasn't feeling sleepy. I'd probably have lain awake on such a mattress as was supplied to the princess in the fairy tale.

I was standing beside the bed when my eye lighted on something like a sliver of silver on the pillow. A minute later I held in my hand a long, thick needle of the kind known as carpet sharps. You know the sort of thing; they're used for repairing carpets and mats, are very powerful, and actually have been used as weapons.

"Nice," said I aloud to the quiet walls. "If I'd turned over and the point (which had been carefully exposed) had got me on a vital spot, they might soon have been singing, 'Now the laborer's task is o'er' on my account." I put the needle in an envelope and got into bed. There would be no more attempts on my life that evening.

"Let me see," said I, still talking aloud, "I must have been out at least ten minutes with Bunty's letter. I hadn't seen the needle before then," but actually I should never be able to prove it hadn't been there when Ross and I came back from the races. Still, straws show the way the wind blows. I became extraordinarily thoughtful.

"Tomorrow, I suppose, there will be something else. And the day after that . . . until the end, whatever that may be."

I might as well keep my mouth shut and my eyes open for those straws that show which way the wind blows. Give a man enough rope, said Crook. I had the cigarette, the twine, the needle. There might be more letters. A wise murderer lies low and does nothing, absolutely nothing. It's when criminals try to be clever, to cover their tracks, that they come to grief. I must wait.

I had to play a waiting game. I realized that, and I could only trust that the luck would be with me.

There would not, I knew, be another attempt on my life that night, so I went to bed without fear, and slept well. I awoke to a shining day and made at once for the bathroom. As I ran down the stairs, however, I saw Ross disappearing along the passage. He looked up as I put my head over the banisters.

"Hello!" said he, rather feebly.

"Sir to you," said I. He vanished rather hurriedly into the bathroom and I went back to my own room. Presently I heard the bathroom door open; I waited a moment, not wanting to meet Ross again; after a minute I gathered my towels and sponge and came out onto the landing. The servant was coming along the corridor and I let her go down before I myself marched triumphantly into the bathroom for my turn. If ever I'm a rich man, said I, to the steamy atmosphere, as I shot the bolt in the door, I shall build a house with a bathroom for every bedroom. Bathrooms are the one serious contribution civilization has made to life, and it's a shame not to take full advantage of it. I had been thinking of the various other ways in which it is possible to bump a man off. Already there had been the gun, the window, the needle. There was death by drowning, death by poison, death by the knife, death under the wheels of an electric train, death by smothering. A lively mind could probably supply other examples, and a fellow can't resolve never to go by tube, take a boat on the river, climb a mountain, have a drink at anyone else's expense. I told myself again I should have to be careful.

I blinked in the steamy atmosphere; the water was heated by an old-fashioned type of tank; I laid my hand against it and found that it still contained a good deal of hot water. The window, I saw, was shut and bolted. I had put down my towels and was unfastening the cord of my dressing gown when someone hammered on the door.

"Mr. Arnold?" yelled Mrs. Judges. "Wanted on the telephone."

"I can't come. I'm in the bath."

"Miss Friar," said the voice.

"Say I'm coming at once," I shouted. Of course, I ought to have rung her up the night before.

Bunty sounded a bit cool. "I suppose you forgot about me," said she.

"I had to go out. It was pretty late when I came back."

"I've got a telephone by the bed. No time would be too late."

"There's only one telephone here, and that's in the hall. You'd wake half the house if you began a conversation at midnight." That wasn't altogether true, but it served.

"How frightfully public. Richard, are you all right?"

"Of course I am."

"There's no 'of course' about it. When are you coming back?"

"I don't know."

"I want you."

"Why? I mean, anything special?"

"Yes." A pause. "I've had another letter."

"The devil you have! When? What does it say?"

"It came this morning. It had a written envelope and—don't be angry—I thought it was an advertisement, so I just threw it in the fire—the envelope, I mean. I always do. But I've got the letter."

I groaned. "It's the envelope we want. Good Lord, Bunty . . . " But there I stopped. What was the use of saying anything? The mischief was done. "What does it say?" I demanded.

"Just, 'You have been warned.' Richard, I'm frantic."

"Darling, I shall be perfectly safe. You must believe me." Some sixth sense made me suddenly turn my head. There was a scuffle of feet, and I saw the maid vanishing down the basement stairs.

"What is it? Richard, are you there?"

"Of course I'm here. It was only someone wanting to telephone. I told him to buzz off. It's all right, nothing's happened."

"But something will."

"I shall be coming back tonight."

"I shan't know a minute's peace until I see you."

We might have gone on like that all day. I hung up the receiver and went upstairs. Half-way up I met Mrs. Judges. At almost the same moment Ross's door opened.

"Good morning," I said. "I wish you'd tell your

henchwoman not to leave her needles in my bed." I spoke purposely rather loud. "Don't you know people have been killed by needles? They run all over the body . . . "

"Drat the girl," said Mrs. Judges. "I never did think she'd be much use. I don't hold with all this class merging, as they call it. Let ladies stay above-stairs—that's what I say. Of course, she's been in trouble . . . "

I stood looking at her, not quite getting the drift of her speech.

"Never done this sort of work before. Been a clerk somewhere. Well, I told her, lady or no lady—though she's not what I'd call a lady—you'll have to empty slops and wash dishes if you stay here. Shouldn't be surprised to hear she was wanted."

"Oh, I don't suggest that the needle was put there on purpose," said I, glancing up to see Ross standing stockstill on the stairs.

When I got upstairs I was furious to find all my things bundled out onto the landing and the bathroom door locked. I thumped on the door. There was a sound of splashing from inside.

"Who the devil's there?" I demanded.

Mrs. Judges popped up at my side like a Jack-in-the-box.

"If you please, sir."

"Look here," I expostulated, "someone's nipped in and taken my bath."

"The bath's common to the 'ole 'ouse," said Mrs. Judges.

"I was in occupation . . . "

"Not when Mr. Fielding got in seemingly, or he wouldn't ha' got in."

"I happened to be called away to the telephone . . . "

"Well, there you are, you see. That's how it was."

"I know that's how it was." I restrained a tendency to shout. "But it isn't how it should be. My clothes were in there . . . "

"Mr. Fielding's my oldest tenant," retorted Mrs. Judges with dignity. "He can't be expected to wait all day for his bath. Not that I expect he'll be long. Very nippy is Mr. Fielding, if he is seventy Wednesday was a week."

Mr. Fielding might be nippy enough in the ordinary way, but he wasn't very nippy that morning. I fumed up and down my room for a quarter of an hour, then I went out onto the landing. I saw Ross coming up again.

"Hello again!" he said.

"Who," I demanded, "is Mr. Fielding?"

"Grand old boy. Mrs. Judges' best beloved. Actually, I believe, he's been here half his life."

"He seems to have spent most that time in the bath."

"In the bath?" Ross looked startled. "You don't mean to say he's there now?"

"I do indeed. He's been there practically ever since you left the room."

"I thought you were going in."

"So I was, but I got called down to the telephone."

"Good Lord! Do you suppose he's all right? I mean, had we better . . . ?"

"I expect he's only soaking. I agree with the stoics, who considered that this wallowing in hot water was the sign of a sensual nature."

"If you'd met old Mr. Fielding you'd find it damned hard to associate him with anything sensual."

"I wish I could meet him—coming out of the bathroom."

"Look here! I don't like the look of this. I believe the old boy's fainted or something. I'm going to bang on the door."

"I don't believe Mrs. Judges will approve."

"I'm going all the same." He walked up to the bathroom door and rapped loudly.

"Excuse me, sir." He put his ear to the crack. "Can't hear a damn' thing," he told me. "You can generally hear a fellow swooshing or something."

"Perhaps he's drying."

"Then why doesn't he answer? I say, sir, you're wanted on the telephone. Look here, Arnold, I'm going to do something about this."

"What?"

"Smash down the door or something."

Mrs. Judges reappeared again like magic. "Pardon me, Mr. Ross, but I could not permit . . . If a gentleman can't have his bath in peace . . . "

"What we're afraid of is it may be his eternal peace."

"Really, Mr. Ross, I'm at a loss to know what you mean."

"I mean that Mr. Fielding has been in that room

for about half an hour, that there isn't a sound, that he doesn't answer when he's called."

By this time I also was pretty apprehensive. I came down and hammered on the panels till they quaked. Mrs. Judges joined in our chorus.

"Mr. Fielding! Mr. Fielding!"

"I tell you what's happened. The old boy's fainted and he's probably slid under the water or something."

"Mr. Ross, how can you?"

"Well, there's clearly something wrong. Look here, we shall have to break the door down. I expect you're insured."

"I don't know what the landlord will say, I'm sure."

"He won't say much, for fear of what the courts will say to him if he turns nasty."

Together Ross and I heaved at the door; the bolt was a flimsy one, but the door took some breaking down.

"Don't smash the panels," implored Mrs. Judges. "I'll get a screwdriver." She hurried downstairs.

"We can't wait for her," I said, for I had by this time a nasty conviction of what we might be going to find. "We've got to get that door open."

I had never realized what a big job smashing down a door can be. We hammered and thrust and banged; Mrs. Judges worked away with a chisel; when at last it gave way, I was precipitated headlong into the room.

"God Almighty!" exclaimed Ross, beginning to choke. I had my handkerchief over my mouth. The window was still closed, and the miasma of the room was poisonous.

"It's that damned heater," cried Ross. "I always told you we ought to have a modern one."

I bent over the prostrate body in the bath; the water was nearly cold, and the unconscious man had turned a dreadful dark blue.

"Escaping fumes," said I. "Get a doctor quickly. Ross and I will get him out. And put on some boiling water. Though I dare say it's too late."

"Good Lord," muttered Ross in my ear, "this is pretty ghastly. Lucky it wasn't you, isn't it?"

"Think so?" said I.

We lugged at that heavy body. I had not known what a dead weight an unconscious body can be. We got him out at last and covered him with towels and carried him, clumsily enough, to his own room, where Mrs. Judges was already putting hot bottles in the bed.

"And I've got a brick in the oven. That's better than any bottle. And the doctor will be here in a minute. What can we do?"

We were applying artificial respiration when the doctor came. "I'll go down," said Ross, but Mrs. Judges forestalled him.

"If you please."

"Can you feel a quiver of life?" Ross asked despairingly.

"Not a quiver."

"Good Lord, who could have anticipated this?"

"You sound like the devil's litany," said I irritably. "Calling on the Lord . . . Hello, here he comes."

The doctor came in, tall, stooping, with pince-nez on his bony nose. He looked at Fielding.

129

"What happened?"

"It was the heater. It must have been an escape. Such a thing's never happened before."

"It's happened hundreds of times before," snapped the doctor. "It's these old-fashioned tanks. Well, the coroner will have something to say."

"The bathroom was all right when I left it," protested Ross.

"I dare say it was, but something must have choked the pipe, driven the fumes into the room. I know this type of heater."

We cleared out presently; he told us there was nothing more we could do. Ross went into his own room. I thought of telephoning Bunty; then another idea struck me. I crept downstairs again to the bathroom. Sounds of heavy breathing told me that someone had preceded me. I went very softly to the doorway. Ross was there, hauling at something.

"Found something?" I asked.

He nearly jumped out of his skin. "Thought I'd just examine the tank," he stammered.

"I expect the police will want to do that."

"There's a stoppage in the pipe. The doctor's right. Good Lord! I wonder how that got there. The fumes must have been pouring into the room, and the window being shut . . . "

"You shut the window, didn't you?"

"I didn't open it. This bathroom's vilely public."

"You might have opened it for the next comer."

"I didn't suppose you wanted to exhibit yourself any more than I did."

130

"You'd better put that thing aside," said I, looking at the obstruction, a bit of dirty rag, that he had pulled out. "The police will want to see it."

"What beats me is how it got there."

"I dare say the police will decide that."

"I suppose so. I think I'll show it to the doctor." He went back to Fielding's room. I heard Mrs. Judges' voice a minute later.

"One of my cleaning rags. I never did. This'll ruin me. Twenty years of letting lodgings and never so much as a couple without marriage lines, and now this."

I waited in the hall for the doctor to come down. I wanted to know whether I should be needed for the inquest. I couldn't help thinking that Marston was a healthier place for me than London at the moment.

The doctor wasn't very long. "Nothing I can do except call the police, and I'm going past the station, so I'll drop in. One thing, I hope this makes the authorities tighten up their regulations about these old heaters. People are always getting choked. Of course he got into the bath and being elderly, and probably drowsy, he became overcome by the fumes."

"Would he know what was happening?"

"I doubt it. His wasn't a particularly good life. I've had him on my hands at various times. If he'd been younger and more alert he might have realized his danger—you can't tell. This practice of soaking in baths is thoroughly bad."

"There, but for the grace of God," said I, and he looked at me in surprise.

"I ought to have been in that bath. I'd dumped my clothes when I was called away to the phone, and the old boy sneaked in the moment my back was turned."

"One man's luck is another man's funeral. Well, I congratulate *you,* anyway. No, you won't be wanted for the inquest. Leave your address in case of emergencies. I must get on. I've got a split appendix and a protracted labor case, and it's hell's delight whether either of them pulls through."

NINE

I WASN'T wanted for the inquest, so I went back to Marston. I rang up Bunty at once.

"Just to reassure you," I told her. "Also, I want to see that letter."

She arranged to meet me at a local cafe. When I had ordered some food, she produced a single sheet of paper. It was like the others in appearance, though the watermark wasn't quite the same.

"Does it help?" she asked.

"I want to keep this."

"Why?"

"I may be able to trace the typewriter. If I can do that the job's done."

When I got back I took out the paper I had typed in Ross' room. The types were identical and so were the watermarks! My next move was simple. I didn't fancy the idea of going to the police with these two bits of paper; it would be better if I could get a letter from Ross, signed by himself, typed on that machine. It ought not to be difficult to obtain such evidence.

I could make the inquest my excuse, and phrase the letter in such a manner that he would be bound to answer it. Then I could produce the two and leave it to the authorities to make the next move. Fisher was a bit skeptical about those letters; I thought I'd like to see him in a white sheet.

The report of the inquest was in the evening papers that came into Marston soon after dinner. I knew there would be a note about the affair; that sort of case never goes unreported, and Ross's connection with it would attract additional attention. The Ross trial had provided the country with one of the criminal sensations of the year.

No one seemed particularly interested in old Fielding. He lived on a pension from a minor civil service post, was about seventy years old, and had been lodging with Mrs. Judges for nearly nine years. He was a bachelor apparently without relatives. There was no reason to suppose he had had any desire to take his own life.

"But there is no particular reason why he should have wished to prolong it?" suggested the coroner.

"He has never spoken of suicide, and there's not an atom of evidence that he ever thought of such a thing. His life wasn't a very good one, but he had a cheerful disposition and seemed very contented with his existence."

"I understand that the rag was found stuffed into the pipe?"

"I didn't see it in position myself." It was the doctor giving evidence.

"Who did?"

"I believe another lodger had removed it before my arrival."

Harry Ross was called, and said that he had gone along to the bathroom to see what had happened; the room had been all right while he was in it a few minutes earlier.

"You didn't think it had been placed there deliberately?"

Ross had hesitated. "Well, I should like to express an opinion."

"You mean it is possible."

"It was wedged, you know. I mean, I had to give a good tug to displace it."

"Did you know Mr. Fielding?"

"Only to talk to casually."

"He never confided in you?"

"He didn't get much chance."

"But he never did?"

"Never."

"So far as you know, he had no financial worries?"

"He didn't tell me about them if he had."

"If you had been told he had taken his own life, you would have been surprised?"

"I don't say that. I really didn't know him well enough. But he seemed pretty cheerful whenever I spoke to him. Besides, it was an odd way to choose."

There seemed to be some difference of opinion about this. The other ways all have disadvantages; poison and firearms aren't in every one's possession, it takes a good deal of nerve to pitch yourself under a train or out of a window, gas ovens aren't available to men in Fielding's position; poison by fumes has become a familiar method, and fumes from a heater can be just as deadly as fumes from the exhaust of a car. Oh, if he'd wanted to take his life this was as effective a way as any.

Mrs. Judges asserted angrily that Mr. Fielding would never have done such a thing to her. It did a lodging house no good to have a death in it, and he was the most considerate of men.

I was surprised that anyone should have suggested suicide; and, of course, nobody thought of murder. Who could conceivably have a motive for murdering old Fielding? The fact that the room ought to have been occupied by myself and not by that unfortunate chap during those critical minutes wasn't generally known.

On the whole, Mrs. Judges came off worst, if you allow that the old man himself was better out of a world where safety's become an obsolete word, and there's nothing much but struggle and disaster to look forward to. She burst into tears in the court when the coroner reprimanded her sternly for retaining so old-fashioned an apparatus in her house.

"Any tank will give off fumes if the pipe gets stopped up," she protested, but she agreed eagerly enough to have a new model substituted immediately. The case had done her no good and lost her her one permanent lodger.

"Coroner condemns old tanks," wrote a facetious reporter.

The jury brought a verdict of death by misadventure, and encouraged by the coroner's remarks added a rider about the landlady.

I couldn't, naturally, prevent Bunty from seeing the paper. I hadn't mentioned old Fielding's death, but she realized at once that there was something fishy about the affair.

"You didn't tell me anything about it," she said accusingly.

"Well, darling, what was the use? I didn't want to alarm you."

"I am alarmed. I'm so awfully alarmed, so frightened that I can't sleep for thinking about it. I wish you'd go into a monastery or something for a bit. It's all very well to talk about coincidences, but you know perfectly well it wasn't anything of the sort."

I couldn't lie about it. I knew damned well it wasn't a coincidence.

"It isn't for much longer," I tried to comfort her.

"That's what I'm afraid of."

"I mean, I believe we are on the right track. And anyhow, all's well that ends well."

"It didn't end well for that old man. And it isn't the end yet."

"It will be soon."

"I'll take care," I promised.

As soon as she had gone I settled down to write to Ross. I wrote in such a manner that I thought he couldn't fail to answer; I wanted the whole affair over and done with as soon as possible. But all I could do was wait, and watch for the postman.

Ross didn't answer the next day, nor the day after that. In fact, before I heard from him something else had happened. Just as there are some lives in which change seems perpetually to operate, so there are some cases in which a fresh development occurs before the implications of the last can be truly assessed. So now something happened that threw all my calculations out of gear.

On the second evening while I was wondering whether the post would bring me my answer, I was informed that a gentleman had called to see me. My first thought was that it might be young Ross in person, but the visitor's name, I was informed, was Wright. It aroused no echo in my mind. Possibly I had met a man of that name, but he had made no impression upon me.

"He says it's private," said the porter.

Instantly my thoughts leaped ahead. The Ross case —it was the one big thing in my life at the moment. I remembered detective novels I had read—men astoundingly disguised appearing at an enemy's house and destroying all incriminating evidence. I thought of Bunty. Then I said, "Send him in." A middle-aged man, rather pale, and walking with his head well forward which gave him a suspicious air, came into the room.

"Mr. Arnold? I know you quite well as a resident, of course, though I don't think we've had the pleasure of meeting."

I suppose I had seen him, but if so he recalled nothing to my mind. Without being precisely negligible he was unimpressive; I could have met him half a dozen times without remembering him.

"I understand you were one of the jurors at the trial of Mrs. Ross."

My heart gave a great leap. "Well?"

"And it was due to you that a unanimous verdict of guilty was not reached?"

"I don't believe it would have been a true verdict."

"No? Well, I'm going to tell you something that may make you change your mind."

I stared. I couldn't imagine what he was going to say.

"You'll think it strange I haven't come forward before, but the fact is I've been convalescing—a long job. Ross actually was killed on my last night at home. I was carted off to a hospital for an immediate operation the next day, and since then I've been abroad. I've only just got back. I never read English papers when I'm abroad, and I hadn't heard of this affair. But now I'm back I can't keep out of it."

"Pardon me, sir, but I don't quite see where you come into it."

"That's what I've come to tell you. I assure you, Mr. Arnold, that if that woman did not actually put the pillow over her husband's face, she is morally as guilty as the man who did."

I drew a long breath. I had been afraid of his disclosure but now it seemed evident that he was one of these fanatics who can't understand that the spirit and letter, in the eyes of the law at all events, are two quite dissimilar things.

"If you mean she egged X on, whoever X may be . . . "

He put up his hand. "Pardon me! I have proof."

"Proof of what?"

"That on the night of her husband's death, at the very time that the outrage must have been committed, Mrs. Ross had a man in that house."

If he had wanted to create a sensation he had succeeded.

"But—how can you possibly know?"

"Because I myself saw him."

There was a little silence after that. At last I said, "Who was he?"

"That I can't tell you. It was too dark for me to see his face. I can only assure you that he was there and that he was her friend and that they spoke to one another in what I can only describe as conspiratorial tones."

"Did you hear what they said?"

"When two people are speaking in a conspiratorial voice they don't usually speak loud enough to be overheard."

I damned him inwardly for a prig. "If you could be a little more explicit, sir . . . "

Rather belatedly I offered him a chair, a cigarette, a drink; he accepted the first two, but not the last.

"It was like this. I told you that I was being removed to a hospital the following day. I am a methodical man and it is my habit to keep my affairs in order, so that it was not necessary for me to make any great disturbance about this matter, although I will confess to you that it came to me as a considerable surprise."

"I don't wonder," I muttered.

"I am speaking, you will understand, of my operation. I had had no reason to suppose that there was anything seriously amiss, and when my physician suggested a second opinion I am afraid I was rather skeptical. I thought it was simply another attempt to take it out of the layman, give another medical man an opportunity to take in a fee. The result of that consultation astounded me. I was told that an immediate operation would be necessary and warned that this might prove unsuccessful, in which case I had only a few more months to anticipate. Naturally I agreed to the operation.

"I agreed, of course, to the operation, but on that particular night I found it difficult to sleep. I dozed off lightly during the early part of the evening, and I awoke with a start to hear the sound of an opening door and then voices. My bed, I should explain, is drawn up under the window, so that by sitting erect and pulling back the curtain I had a very good view of the front garden of the next door house, which, as it happens, belongs—belonged rather to Mr. Ross. Being awakened my curiosity was mildly aroused. I leaned forward, and it was then that I heard the voices. As I have said, I could not distinguish a word. I did however realize that the speakers were a man and a woman. A moment later I saw a figure go down the path and open the gate. As I have said, the fellow was talking as if he were on a platform, I could not see his face."

"But you assume automatically that he was the murderer?"

"Why has he not come forward?"

"He's very likely terrified that other people will leap

141

to your conclusion. I'm not at all sure I shouldn't be myself."

"An innocent man has nothing to fear."

"Tell that to the police and listen to them laugh. An innocent man has every bit as much to fear as the guilty. In fact, more, because he can't build up alibis, as guilty men generally do. Besides, think of the construction everyone would instantly put on his relationship to Mrs. Ross."

"And would they be wrong?"

"You've no reason to assume they would be right. People should be judged on facts, not on public opinion."

"There cannot be a clear sequence of facts in a case like this one. No one commits murder in public. You're bound to rely to a large extent on circumstantial evidence."

"And why has she said nothing about it, if he's guilty?"

"Surely the reason is obvious."

I could think of nothing on the spur of the moment to reply to that. The information he had given me had been a blow between the eyes. I had never thought of this. Naturally, if this story became public property, the whole world would say what he was saying with such brutal disregard for my feelings at this instant.

"Naturally she wouldn't speak of him," my companion went on. "It wouldn't help her; in fact, it would effectually sign her death warrant. I have no doubt she is still hoping there may be another sentimentalist on the next jury who will refuse to face the facts. When she *is* found guilty, then see what she does. That'll be the test." He spoke in a positively gloating voice. You know, it's astonishing that murder should be the one crime for which the death penalty is exacted.

I was, as I admit, filled with consternation at this new development. Once the fellow went to the police with his information, it seemed to me we were dished. It would be the crowning touch. Then I wondered if he had already handed in his piece.

"What do the authorities think?" I asked him.

"I haven't been to the police yet. I thought it fairer to warn you of the facts."

"Hoping I'd drop out, haul down my colors, in short?"

"It's the duty of every citizen to help the police in their search for a criminal."

"According to you and the police you've got your criminal."

"This is additional evidence. I should be an accessory after the event if I said nothing about it."

"You haven't got any evidence," I objected. "You simply heard and saw someone walk away from the house that night. That's all your 'evidence' amounts to."

"It isn't all it would amount to by the time the police had done with it."

"My point exactly. Look here, Mr. Wright, will you do me a favor?"

"What's that?"

"Don't do anything for twenty-four hours. By the way," a new thought struck me, "how can you be sure it was that night?"

"I tell you, I was going to the hospital the next morning. You can check up on that date."

"But it might conceivably be the night before and you've got confused. After all, it was some time ago."

"I keep a diary."

I might have known it. He was one of those inconceivably conceited and pompous asses who consider their activities important enough to be recorded.

"Of course, the police would ask for that."

"Of course, they would. I see. Well, will you do what I ask?"

"And take no action for twenty-four hours? How will that help you?"

"I'd like to know what Mrs. Ross would say."

"Give her a chance to concoct a story, in short?"

I shrugged impatiently. "What the hell kind of story do you think she can concoct now? She can't even get in touch with this man; all her correspondence is examined. But there may be some reason . . . "

"She can tell it to the police."

"The police won't take any further action. They're convinced of her guilt. They won't thank you for wiping their eye the way you're trying to. But there may be some reasonable explanation. . . . No, I don't know what it is any more than you do. But if this story gets about it won't be recognizable by the time the trial comes on. Give me that respite. It can't make any difference to you."

Well, he agreed. I don't think he wanted to, but he did. He said he was going to be pretty busy the next day anyhow. He had to see the doctor and go along

144

to his office. There was business he'd had to postpone for weeks. I got him out as soon as I could, which wasn't very early, and then I sat back and wiped my forehead. This was worse than anything I had supposed. I couldn't conceive of any explanation that could be offered that would pass muster.

Of course, I told myself, supposing this fellow was right, that wasn't any proof that the man was guilty. But if he wasn't, then there would be a hundred times more reason to suppose that she was. He was her lover—it went without saying that everyone would suppose that. He had gone to see her for some particular reason. Irene Cobb had said that Mrs. Ross went out immediately after a scene with her husband. Why?

The answer to that was easy. I imagined the story as it would spread through the village. Teddy Ross had told her that he knew the truth, that he proposed to act. She went out to telephone to her lover. She brought the lover home, one or other of them murdered Ross. The only thing that would remain in doubt would be the identity of the guilty man.

Suddenly I knew I wasn't going to see her, as I had told Wright I meant to do. It would serve my purpose better to go back to town and see Harry. It would be dangerous, but everything connected with this affair was dangerous. I would see him, tell him Wright's story, note his reactions. He might try and make a getaway— no, he wouldn't do that. But did he realize that I was gradually building up a case against him?

I resolved to go to town in the morning. I lay awake a good deal that night, making plans. I ought, probably, to warn Crook what I was doing. He wouldn't like my butting in—I've always hated a goat, he would say—but this was the most important thing in my life. It was only one of a number of "cases" to him, just as a man's life is just a case to a doctor, but the whole of this world and the next to the woman who loves him. All Crook cared about was getting his fees paid and not being made to look a fool.

TEN

THERE wasn't any time to waste; I caught an early train next morning and went to see Harry Ross. I went there first, in case Crook tried to prevent my going at all, and I didn't say a word to Bunty before I left, in case she wanted to come with me and make my job harder than it was anyhow. In my own mind I was haunted, as I had been haunted ever since the opening of the case, with the fear that perhaps there had been something between Mrs. Ross and her stepson. Naturally she would deny it; naturally, so would he. But if I could prove that that relationship had existed —what then? I hated the idea so much that I could almost persuade myself it couldn't be true. Almost but not quite.

It was a day to discourage the most stout-hearted. A bleak early morning turned by ten o'clock into an uncompromising drizzle; a sharp wind blew pieces of newspaper around the corners of the streets. Of course, Harry Ross was out. I went up to my room, stared out of the window, remembered what had happened when I was last here, conjectured what might happen this time, and finally, realizing that this was an opportunity that might not come again, slipped down to the next floor and rapped on Harry Ross's door. Naturally, no one answered me. I rapped again. Then I turned the handle and went in. The first thing I looked for was the typewriter that stood under the window. But before I could cross the room I heard his foot on the stair. I turned quickly as he opened the door.

"Oh, here you are there. Thank heaven for that."

He looked at me in surprise. "What's up?"

"I'll tell you. I don't know whether you'll be able to help."

"I don't either." He sounded ungracious. "By the way, I'd just written to you."

"Oh? You might let me have the letter." He rootled among a pile of papers, said casually, "You don't mind about the envelope, do you?" and handed it to me. I took it without looking at it.

"What's this other thing?" he went on. I thought today his manner was more suspicious than usual. He was as jumpy as a buck-rabbit.

I told him what Wright had said. I saw the color drain away from his face.

"Who was the fellow?" he asked sharply.

"Wright couldn't see him clearly enough to identify him. But you may be sure the powers that be will leave no stone unturned to get him. You do realize what this means, don't you?" I never took my eyes off his face.

"What does it mean?" he mumbled.

"Well—either that he did it and she knows he did

or she did it herself. There is no other alternative."

There was a long and awkward silence. Ross moved over to the table, where he began to play aimlessly with a long blue pencil, hitting at the scattered sheets.

"Yes," he said at last, "there's one other thing. My father may have been dead when those two came into the house."

"There isn't a jot of evidence to support such a view."

"There isn't a jot of evidence to support anything. I must say I don't know why you came to me with such a story. I can't help you. I don't know anything."

"You can't offer any suggestions as to who the fellow may have been?"

I watched him very closely. He shook his head; there wasn't even any color in his lips.

"I never knew anything about her private affairs, except that she wasn't happy with my father."

"She never—this is important—she never dropped any hint about some other man?"

"Not to me."

"It's significant that she didn't speak of this at the trial."

"Well, you ass, how could she? It would be about the worst thing she could do. You don't ask a man in to have a drink at eleven-thirty in a cathedral town like Marston, particularly when your husband's just told you he's going to cut you out of his will."

"That may have been just why—sheer defiance. She strikes me as being just that type of woman."

"It would be a damn silly thing to do."

"She appears to have done it. I'm afraid it's going

to be difficult to disprove this fellow's existence. Wright has it all written up in his diary, and you can't very well suggest that's faked. For one thing, he has no motive, and for another there will be dozens of subsequent entries."

He turned on me then like a dog that has been teased too long.

"How the hell do you expect me to help you?"

"I see you can't. But when we're up against things as we are at the moment you can't afford to leave any loophole unsearched."

"Does one search loopholes?" he wondered vaguely. "You know, I suppose there couldn't be anything in it? No, no, of course not. If she'd wanted to be free of Father she had only to walk out on him."

"A widow decently provided for is a horse—a mare, rather—of a very different color from a woman living apart from her husband, without means. She'd given up wage-earning nearly a dozen years previously. I'm only giving you the official, the popular point of view."

"Look here, you say she ought to have told everyone about the visitor straight away. But she didn't realize it wasn't natural death at first, till that wretched Cobb woman upset everybody's apple-cart."

"Who says that?"

That stopped him. "I see. Good heavens, it's a pretty grim kettle of fish. You'd better get her story next, hadn't you?" He walked irresolutely up and down the room. "Damned interfering old codger!" he muttered.

"I'm afraid we can't shut his mouth."

150

He swung around fiercely. "Can't we? My God, why should these outsiders be allowed to interfere? All the same, isn't it a question of his word against hers?"

"I doubt if that helps her much. He hadn't any motive for writing in his diary a thing that wasn't true. He couldn't know your father would be found dead next day."

"I suppose not. Oh, God, what's to be done now?"

He couldn't help me. I hadn't expected that he would, but his evident distress was dismaying. I went up to my room, and compared the two specimens of typescript. "Now," I thought, "I've got you, my fine chicken."

A minute later I sat down, dazed. The two types were totally dissimilar!

I had been so certain that, in my own mind, I was already evolving phrases for the police when I showed them the letter and the unsigned warning. This took all the sawdust out of my system. I looked again. I knew those two were alike, I knew that letter to Bunty had been typed on young Ross's machine. But what was the good of my saying so? If I produced my own wretched specimen they'd say, "What proof is there that that was typed in Ross's room?" It was a queer sort of story to tell, anyway.

I got up presently and went downstairs. In the hall I met Mrs. Judges.

"I wanted to ask you, sir," she began, "about that room. . . ."

"You want it?"

"No, it isn't that. It's Mr. Fielding's room. I was

thinking you might have a friend coming to London —I don't like to take people in promiscuous, and some of these newspaper chaps that come here—well, they don't seem to have any sense of decency. Goodness knows, nobody ever took any notice of the poor old man while he was alive. They might let him rest in peace."

"If I hear of anyone," I promised vaguely.

"I can't really afford to have my rooms empty," Mrs. Judges explained.

"None of the others are going, are they?"

"Not Mr. Kenward. He's the safe kind. Not likely to get married in a hurry, either."

"Mr. Ross isn't talking of getting married, is he?"

"N-no. But he's not settled-like. Talking of another job, wanting more conveniences, though what he means by that goodness only knows, and I don't think he does, because I asked him."

"Going upstage, is he?"

"Well, he's been getting a new suit and a new machine—"

"What?" I grabbed her by the arm. "Did you say a new typewriter?"

"That's what I said." She sounded surprised, outraged almost.

"Well, he is going up in the world. You don't buy those for the price of an old postage stamp."

"He said it was offered him cheap and he could make something off the old one."

"What did he do with the old one?"

"Sold it. He advertised it in the shop at the end of

the road. Four pounds he was asking for it."

"The shop at the end of the road?" I repeated.

"Yes, Smithson's, the stationers. You pay sixpence a week and they put a card in their showcase. He sold it right away."

"It seems a cheap form of advertisement."

I thought that Smithson's might be able to help me. I went along there at once, but the young woman behind the counter was singularly unamenable.

"An advertisement? About a typewriter? Yes, I believe we did have one. It isn't in the case any more, is it?"

"No, I understand the machine was sold."

"Well, then, of course, it wouldn't be in the case."

"I thought you might remember who bought the machine."

"Oh, we shouldn't know that."

"Do they buy them through you?"

"Oh, no, through the advertisement."

"But don't you get a commission? Don't you get anything for exhibiting the advertisement?"

"Sixpence a week we charge."

"And don't you keep any record of your advertisements?"

"Yes, we have a book. I could tell you who put the advertisement in."

"I know that. When was it put in?"

She looked up the date. "Only two days ago. It went right away. The gentleman came in the very next evening and said it was sold."

"He didn't say who'd bought it?"

ANTHONY GILBERT

"Oh, no."

"It was a big machine, wasn't it?"

"Well, I never saw it. . . ."

"Of course not." There was nothing to be learned from her, but it occurred to me that I might be able to find out something from whoever removed it from Ross's rooms. These full-size machines can't be carried under your arm. They have to be taken away in a taxi or by Carter Paterson. I went back to Mrs. Judges.

"I think I'll catch the late train," I said. "By the way, is Mr. Ross in now?"

"He went out soon after you did. Said he'd be late."

"What does late mean?"

"Well, sometimes it means he's out all night. He goes to the House of Commons sometimes. I ask him if he thinks he knows enough to make laws."

"Does he want to stand?"

"Why not? Six hundred a year out of our pockets and do as much or as little as you like."

"Does he often go to the House?"

"Has done lately, goodness knows why. Or says he does. I couldn't tell you, of course. If you ask me, these young men want a proper job, not just hanging about and working when they feel inclined. Marry young and have a family to keep and you've no time to get into mischief. That's what I say. No money, either."

"And half the time the state keeps your family," I agreed. "Look here, I wanted to ask you about that typewriter. The one Mr. Ross sold."

"What do you think I know about it?"

154

"You don't know who bought it?"

"A young woman."

"Did she come here and take it?"

"She did. In a taxi. Well, I thought, if you can afford a taxi you might afford a new machine."

"A new machine costs a bit over thirty pounds."

"He's become quite rich all of a sudden."

"Looks like it. He didn't lose any time getting in the new one."

"Oh, that come in before the other went out. That only went last night."

I didn't like to pump her further. I could probably learn what I wanted to know from the neighboring taxi stand. I asked if I could phone for a taxi and she told me the number. I rang up and when the taxi came, told it to drive me to the Beverley Hotel, which wasn't more than five minutes distant. When we got there I alighted and said, "Look here, I want to trace the driver of a taxi that called at that house last night and collected a young woman and a typewriter."

"Not me," said the driver at once.

"It was one of the cabs on your rank."

"You'd better come back and ask the others."

"I must just see about a room here," said I, "and then I'll come along."

I went into the hotel, asked if a Mrs. Hillier was staying there, was told she wasn't expected, and came out again. I got into the cab and was driven back to the rank. I was lucky in finding a man almost at once who remembered the fare.

"Do you remember where you took the machine?"

"To Helmsley Mansions. Know them? Little bachelor flats, they call 'em. Well, that's as may be, but you can't 'ardly swing a cat in the rooms."

"Have you been there, then?"

"Carried the typewriter in, up in the lift first floor. Carried it down from the room in Vane Street, the fare was two and three and she gave me 'arf a crown. And then they go making jokes in the papers about drivers 'aving bad manners. The Angel Gabriel 'ud make a long nose at some of the fares we get."

I thanked the fellow and went off to find Helmsley Mansions. A bus took me within a stone-throw, and I looked at the board in the hall. The mansions were narrow-chested affairs, with two doors to each landing. The first floor flats were occupied by a Mr. and Mrs. Breese and a Miss Mortimer.

I walked up the stairs and stopped in front of the second flat. Pinned on the wall by the bell was a printed card:

ELSIE MORTIMER

TYPEWRITING

That was a bit of luck. I pushed the bell. The girl who answered it matched the building perfectly. She was flat-chested, sallow, uninspiring, wearing glasses with bright green rims, and a frock she might have made herself or picked up at a second-hand dress shop. Her sandy hair was short and badly dressed.

"Miss Mortimer? I was visiting some people upstairs and on the way down I happened to see your card. I'm a novelist and I have two or three important letters to get off tonight. Is it possible to dictate them to you straight onto the machine? They're urgent and I have to go out of London in about half an hour."

"Of course." I should think I was her first client that day. She overdid her casual air, as she led me through the stuffy, unappetizing little hall and took me into the sort of room you'd expect from her appearance. There was a typewriter on the table.

"How many carbons?"

"Oh, one. Just for reference."

"And the address?"

"Nightingale Chambers, Pall Mall. What kind of machine is that?"

"A Regal. As a matter of fact, it's a new one. I only bought it yesterday."

"They're always bringing out new models," said I carelessly.

"This isn't a new one. It's often better to get a really good rebuilt machine. Then you know it's been properly overhauled. Some of the new kinds they keep putting on the market—they're simply chronic."

I made no comment. I spun out three letters, one dealing with film contracts, and I saw her eyes widen and then grow round. When she ripped the paper out of the machine she said, "Awf'ly interesting being an author, isn't it? I've always thought I'd like to write."

"I expect you haven't the time," said I smoothly.

"That's just it. I seem to be on the rush all day, and of course, at night I'm too tired."

"And then, of course, you have to have something to write about."

"Do you write up the people you meet?" she chattered on. "I expect you do, and they never know it."

Everybody asks an author that, most of them pretend they'd hate to find themselves in a book, and practically all of them believe they will be anyway. I read the letters, asked what I owed for them, carried them off. I had brought the slip of paper that Bunty had received. I checked up under a lamp at a street corner. It was all right. The type was the same. She had fitted a new ribbon, but there were identification marks no one could overlook. I shoved the papers back in my pocket, yelled to a passing taxi and caught my train by a fraction of a minute.

ELEVEN

ON THE WAY back the thoughts raced around and around my head. They went so fast they became confused in my own mind, and I had to put the brake on and take them one by one. I tried to rid myself of all personal prejudice, look at this thing with the colorless indifference of Scotland Yard.

Bunty—and others—got anonymous letters of a threatening nature. The threats are put into practice and by sheer bad luck—or good; it depends whose point of view you take—they don't come off. A final letter is received. Then the typewriter on which they were written changes hands. No reason for such a thing, there was nothing wrong with the machine. Ross hadn't even bought a new one, but he'd got rid of the old in double quick time. His version was that he'd been offered a much better machine dirt cheap. Well, perhaps he had, but it all fitted in uncommonly well.

Now I could prove that the last letter Bunty had was typed on that machine. The inference was that the others had been typed on that one too. That couldn't be proved because we hadn't got the others any longer. But this would be enough. The police, I supposed, would argue that the letters weren't just a way of passing the time; they meant something, and the fact that they had been directed against me pointed to the fact that the author was anxious to see me out of the way. And there could only be one reason for that, the fact that I was busying myself with finding a substitute on the gallows for Viola Ross. It all seemed to fall into place. I wondered whether the police would be any more satisfied with young Ross's explanation of how he spent the evening of the fatal night than I was. I was home when it occurred to me that it wasn't going to be any too good for Mrs. Ross, either way. Because suppose we could show that young Harry was the man in the house that evening, still it didn't exonerate her. I went to bed brooding like a hen. Whichever way I added it up the answer came wrong.

I dozed a bit, I think, and suddenly sat bolt upright with my heart going like a trip-hammer. You know those nightmares when you sit up in a pitch dark room and know you aren't alone. Everyone has experienced that sensation, and it's pretty horrible. I looked at my watch. I thought it must be far later, but it was barely midnight. Words were rushing through my mind. "Pity we can't put that old codger out of the way."

Who had said them? Automatically I was out of bed and reaching for my trousers. What had I said to Harry Ross? "The old fool sits up half the night scribbling his damned diary." And in his diary he had recorded the fact that a man was with Viola Ross on the night that her husband was murdered. I fastened my collar with shaking hands. Wright had promised not to go to the police for twenty-four hours. That meant the secret was safe until the morning. After that he became a danger—to whom? To the man who was involved in Teddy Ross's death. And I —I had been up to London, put my head in the lion's mouth, told Harry what had happened. "Pity we can't put that old codger out of the way." I pulled on my coat, opened the door of my flat, let myself out of the building. I was thinking, "If anything were to happen to Wright before he went to the police, who would know about that late night visitor?" I should know and so would Ross, and which of us would be likely to come forward?

I walked quickly down the street, avoiding the brighter side, and turned into Little David Lane. That was a short cut to the avenue where the Rosses had had a house and where Wright lives now. As I went I told myself that I was a fool to be so perturbed. But I went on just the same. I turned down the lane out of Romany Street and went along under the shadow of the wall. Wright's house was next door, and beyond that was a house that had been for some time untenanted. I gently pushed open the door in the wall. If the house were dark . . .

The house was not dark. In a lower room the light was burning. Curtains had been pulled across the windows but these did not quite meet and a bright bar of gold advertised the fact that life was alert there.

Pulling the door to behind me, I stole up the path. My position there was an invidious one. If I were suddenly discovered, as I might well be if Wright or whoever was the occupant of that room came to look out of his window, it might sound a little strange to say, "As a matter of fact, I think Mr. Wright may be going to be murdered shortly. I'm here on chance." My rubber-soled shoes made no sound on the path; I crept nearer and nearer. If the curtains were suddenly parted I was done for. There wasn't an atom of shelter in sight.

Nobody appeared, however; there wasn't a breath of life in the garden; the wind had dropped, the branches never stirred, even the leaves looked as though they were painted against a black velvet sky. I went nearer and nearer. The window itself was guarded by a barrier of thickly-grown laurels that had been cut to a flat surface, as solid and unyielding as a table. I tiptoed up to these and peered through the golden slit. Wright was in the room; he was seated at a table writing hard; his head was down, his attention was focused on what he did. He might have been a machine sitting there, oblivious to everything but his own job of the moment. He never seemed to halt for a word; on and on the pen drove. That steady industry enthralled me. He was writing on a pad of manuscript paper, and as he finished each page he tore it off and laid it aside. He seemed to have a good deal to say. It occurred to me that he might be writing his diary; then—more ominous! and my heart began its irregular trip-hammer beat at the idea—he might be making out his statement for the police. He had given me twenty-four hours, and the time was up. I stood there like a man of stone.

Life suddenly invaded my consciousness; a wind blew from nowhere, rustling the leaves of a chestnut tree close by; a cloud sailed over the face of the moon; all the light around me was blotted out. In the darkness an owl hooted, so close, so unearthly, that involuntarily I started back. A twig snapped under my feet; I felt the sweat prickling my forehead. But the man in the room paid no heed. On, on drove that relentless pen; I told myself I could hear the scratching of the nib.

At last Wright laid the pen aside. He gathered the loose sheets, pinned them together, then settled back in his chair and began to read. I asked myself what the devil I thought I was doing there. I began to hate that man on the other side of the glass, with his deliberation, his assumption of his own importance, the aggressive nose, the streaks of black hair plastered smugly across the gleaming scalp. I remembered his voice when he spoke of Viola Ross—the sanctimonious sinner—with his heart burning with uncharity, his eagerness to cast if not the first at least the heaviest stone he could unearth. I could have strangled him where he sat.

He was through at last; he pinned the sheets together, stood up, took an envelope from a drawer and folded the papers. Then he moved; the silence was so intense again that I heard the scratch of a match.

"He's going to smoke," thought I. "Heavens above, he's making a night of it." A fleeting idea that he might, after all, be going to destroy that portentous document, died at a second thought. The Wrights of this earth do not treat their affairs with such levity. He was out of my sight now; I just clung there, frozen, despairing, full of doubt.

What happened was entirely unexpected. I had been waiting for perhaps three or four minutes. Then the silence of the night, of the house, of the whole sleeping atmosphere was shattered by the sound of a shot. I was so staggered I didn't move, I didn't cry out. I don't think at first I quite believed I had heard the sound. At length I put my hand to my head as if to reassure myself that it was still on my shoulders. That movement galvanized me into life. Here was I interloping on the premises of a man I had met once and then not in the happiest circumstances, while on the other side of the glass was—what? The idea that he might have been murdered didn't go through my mind. I didn't believe anyone could have entered the room without my being aware of it. I was as certain as I was standing there that Wright for some reason I couldn't fathom had taken his own life. The letter he had written would probably explain why.

The obvious course now was to go while the going was good, but I couldn't do it. It was a question of rival dangers. I might get back home without discovery, but I couldn't tear myself away until I knew the nature of the letter he had been writing in that lonely house.

About this juncture it occurred to me as strange that the shot had aroused no one. However sound a sleeper you are, the atmosphere should be so much disturbed by this untoward happening that the truth will penetrate the most absorbing dream, shatter the most complete unconsciousness. I leaned a little closer trying to see farther into the room. Surely that door would fly open, someone would come tearing in. At the mere thought I dropped below the level of the laurel bushes. But though I crouched there, alternately burning and chilled by turns, nothing happened. I straightened myself and stepped back. The houses on either side were unmoved; that, of course, was natural. I had momentarily forgotten that neither was occupied. Beyond that the sound of the shot might not carry. Before I returned, at whatever risk, I had to discover what had happened inside that room. If there was anyone in the house he had remained undisturbed. If a man could sleep through that distraction he ought not to hear the minor sound of a man breaking in.

I pressed myself desperately against the solid phalanx of the laurels. I heard twigs snapping, something scratched my face. I pushed forward. Now my hands were on the framework of the window, now I was touching the sash. It had been opened several inches; by pulling down the top still farther I could open it at the bottom. I made two or three ineffectual attempts, then I was successful; I wormed my way over the edge, and then I was in the room.

There was no living creature there besides myself, but on the carpet by the fireplace, that had been invisible from my position outside, something sprawled on the carpet, something dark, senseless, from whose shattered head a dark substance oozed. I flung the door open, took a step into the hall before I realized that at all costs I must conceal my presence here from every living thing. I closed the door again and came back to the body. The thing that had been Oscar Wright had not been a particularly pleasant sight in life; in death he nauseated me. The bullet had torn its way through his skull and smashed into the wall by the side of the fireplace; the head was shot to pieces; there was blood everywhere.

My immediate desire was somehow to conceal that bloody head. A pile of newspapers lay in a corner of the room and I had stooped to take one of these when I realized that I must do nothing, nothing, to indicate that anyone had entered there since the tragedy.

If I could have realized the position in cold blood I should have been crazy with fear. As it was there was an element of macabre unreality that saved my reason. If anyone appeared I'd say I had heard a shot, had been unable to attract attention and had entered in desperation.

The sooner I got out of this room the better. Propped against a monumental clock on the mantelshelf I saw the fatal letter. It was addressed to Colonel Hyde, who was, I knew, the local coroner, a retired R.A.M.C. man and a fine golfer. The envelope had been sealed with Wright's own seal. On the table nearby lay a box with balls of sealing wax, a spoon, a candle and a box of wax vestas. That explained the striking of the match; he had wanted to melt the wax.

I wondered at the precision a man will display within

an ace of a self-inflicted death. I took the letter between my fingertips. It would be hopeless to try to open that and then reseal it so that it didn't look as though it had been tampered with. Either I must let it go and take my chance or I must open it. The fact that it wasn't addressed to the police and that there was no sign of any other letter, coupled with his undertaking not to inform the authorities until the twenty-four hours had expired, convinced me that that long document I had watched him write contained some fatal reference to Viola Ross. I stood there, irresolute. I didn't want to appear in this affair; it would, indeed, by disastrous for us all if I did. But dared I take that chance? Looking over the table, I saw the diary, a handsome, extravagantly bound book in green leather. I laid the letter aside and looked at the pertinent entry. Oh, that was clear enough. The whole history of the visit of X to the Ross's house was detailed with a clarity and a regard for detail that even Scotland Yard couldn't hope to better. I turned the pages forward. Had he spoken of his visit to me the previous day? He had, of course. "Called on this fellow Arnold, to convince him of the futility of continuing this campaign to whitewash Mrs. Ross. Another case of hopeless infatuation. The woman is a murderess and deserves to die. My evidence will go a considerable way to showing that she was also an adultress. I have no sympathy for such, nor do I consider the law should be softened on their account. The female of the species is more deadly than the male."

At that instant it seemed to me that if Viola Ross

were guilty of everything of which she was accused, she
was a far less contemptible creature than what now
lay on the carpet at my feet. For the first time it occurred to me to wonder why he should have taken his
own life. Such a thought, I was convinced, had never
been in his mind when he came to see me the night
before. The letter, of course, would tell me, but if
that was all it would tell me I didn't want to incur
the colossal risks of opening it. I stood there a long
time, my will weakening. Then I slit the envelope. I
could readdress the stuff, writing the name in a script
lettering, reseal it and lean it against the clock. It was,
as Crook would say, all Lombard Street to a china
orange against the powers that be querying the writing
on the outside.

The early part of the letter dealt with the ethics of
suicide, and was extremely dull, except possibly to a
psychologist; I didn't give a damn about the fellow's
immortal soul; you could have crammed it into a pea-
pod anyway. The upshot of the whole thing was that
he had realized his disease was incurable; the operation
and the long convalescence could effect temporary relief; but it would be an affair of repetition, one operation after another, and each time the period of relief
would be shorter.

Wright wrote that he had a horror of sickness, that
the work a man could effect in such circumstances was
negligible, and explained that he was, therefore, "getting out" while he was able to do so, and before he
was regarded as a chronic nuisance by his little world.

"I am neither a child nor an imbecile, and I wish

to place on record my intense resentment at the manner in which the doctors and specialists have treated me. I placed my affairs in order on the eve of my operation, and I think I may claim to have left my executors an easy task." He continued in this strain for some time; I read on impatiently. I wondered whether my safest plan wouldn't be to destroy the letter outright, but a moment's thought convinced me that a fellow like the deceased would never be satisfied to go out quietly and anyone who knew him would realize that.

On the last page of the interminable screed came the reference I sought. The word diary leaped up from the third line. "I have kept a meticulous record of my sensations, progress and relapses," he wrote. "These may be of interest to the medical profession. In any case I bequeath them this diary in the hope that it may aid them to deal with other men more expeditiously than they have done with me." There was no mention of Viola Ross anywhere. I supposed that his colossal preoccupation with himself had driven all thought of her from his mind. Nevertheless, I was glad I had opened the envelope.

Again I considered the expediency of destroying the letter, but even if I did so the diary remained. Indeed, it would be examined with particular care, since it would be the sole indication of the fellow's mind. I laid the letter down and picked up the diary again. The final entry had been made that evening. It recorded the visit to the doctor, his own dilemma, his decision. "I am about to write an explanatory statement to Colonel Hyde," he had said. No, I couldn't destroy the letter. The only alternative, therefore, was to destroy those pages in the diary that were relevant to the Ross case, and it remained to be seen whether this could be done without arousing suspicion.

A brief examination assured me that it could not. There were other entries on the reverse side of the sheet whose absence would be instantly detected. I dared not destroy the book, I could conceive of no place where it might be safely hidden. It was then that the memory returned to me of the classic author of old who, falling asleep in the middle of his work, awoke to find that an overturned candle had burned through a great bulk of his manuscript. With incredible perseverance he had "patched" the separate pages, but in this case there would be no one to do that because no one would know the nature of the missing record. I opened the diary a few pages before the ominous entry, I relighted the candle Wright had used for sealing the letter, I let it fall on the sheet. Then I stood watching. I wanted to be sure that it would not simply char the topmost page and smoulder out in a brown stain.

The plan worked famously. The page slowly crumbled under my eyes. I left it there; it could burn the whole place down if it liked. I resealed the letter, printed the name of Colonel Hyde on the envelope, and looked around to see whether I had left any fatal traces of my presence there. Just as I was about to leave I remembered the damaging entry at the end of the diary. This, I found, could be dealt with by the simple process of cutting out the offending sheet, removing its blank counterpart, and giving the impression that, since he was leaving so long a statement for the benefit of the coroner, Wright had not thought it necessary to make the usual entry in the diary.

Getting out of the room was an even more ticklish job than breaking in. Recalling every detective story I had ever read, I roughly smeared the brass candlestick so that no individual fingerprint could be discerned. To wipe it completely clean might arouse suspicion. I did not know that the average author pays far more attention to technical trivialities than the flesh and blood policeman and, as often as not, misses the larger issues in so doing. The bushes were like inimical witnesses; they caught me in every direction. I heard the rip of material as my coat caught on a particularly obstinate bough, but it was too dark for me to make any investigation.

The moon was again hidden, for which I was thankful, but it had its reverse side. For now it was so dark that even when I was in the garden I could not distinguish the path from the border of flowering plants that edged it. I made an uncertain step in the darkness. I dared not light a match, and I was afraid of stumbling and thus attracting attention. Now that the hardest part of the task was accomplished my fears rushed upon me an hundredfold. To be caught now! I took an incautious step and felt my foot sink into soft earth. I realized that I had plunged into the flower bed. All now was lost. My footprint would be discovered in the morning, it would immediately be identified as mine, most probably I should be accused of murdering Wright and forging his confession. I went down on my hands and knees and tried to smooth over the earth with my hands. I might not be able to conceal the fact that someone had come this way last night, but at least I could with luck make it impossible to prove who that interloper was.

After that I went more carefully than ever, so carefully that I fell over the edge of the lawn on the other side and bruised my knee. There was a stiff feeling about one cheek, and I thought most probably I had grazed the skin, and should have to think up some story for the morning. I went inch by inch down a path that seemed as long as the road leading to the Perfect Day. More than once I thought I must be going around in a circle. Once I went down on my knees and, chancing discovery, struck a match in my cupped hands. The momentary flicker, that was all I got before it went out, showed me that I was halfway down the path and no more. On then I went.

At last I reached the gate. My hand moved over the surface roughened by time and exposure. I found the latch. I lifted it as though upon the faintest trickle of sound my whole life depended. I stood there with the latch in my fingers fearful of pulling the door wide lest something lurked on the farther side, hungry to entrap me. I pulled it toward me inch by inch. The blackness was taking strange shapes; I could swear I saw anonymous figures flit by me; I felt their breath whistling among my hair. Once I knew that a hand had brushed my face. I dared not pull the door wide.

I had walked up this path like a free man; I went

out like a hag-ridden creature of legend, who knows he is dicing with death and that the dice are loaded. There was no one in the lane, but here a flicker of light shone, and I could make my way more readily to the entrance of the main street. Here again terror overwhelmed me. The authorities had arranged for a policeman to be on duty at a point near this spot, and though naturally he did not stand stockstill, but moved to and fro and around the corner, the certainty shook me that as I emerged I should find him staring at me in amazement, in pardonable curiosity. I stood there, my hand over my heart, that seemed as though it would leap out of my breast. At last in a fever of apprehension I took a step forward; with my head bent I walked rapidly around the corner and up the street; I would not look up to see whether the policeman were there or not, but I adopted a slightly dragging walk, as though I were lame. At the top of the street I flung a single glance over my shoulder. There was no one there; then I heard regular footsteps and knew that in another moment the man on duty would appear. I turned another corner and knew that so far as he was concerned I was safe.

I reached the block of flats without meeting a soul. We had no night porter, and I had long ago managed to get a door-key to the heavy outer doors. I opened these carefully, found the hall in darkness, struck a match to prevent my falling over a rug or a chair pushed out of place, and went in. There wasn't a light burning anywhere; the transoms over the two flat doors were as black as though blinds had been drawn across them.

I opened my own door, shut it noiselessly and within five minutes was undressed and in bed. Now that I was safe I began to know the desire of any man in a tight corner to establish an alibi. I wondered whether I would ring up the telephone operator and complain that for the past hour I had been disturbed by wrong numbers; then I reflected that it was just possible that someone had telephoned me and there had been no one to take the call. It would be better to do nothing. It was Crook's advice. "Be bloody, bold and resolute and keep your mouth shut."

TWELVE

THE next day I remained indoors working at a novel. But at about twelve-thirty I went down to The Lucky Chance; they serve a decent lunch there for half a crown. There were always two or three confirmed clients in the place at that hour. One of them was Harry Powis, whose nickname was *The Daily Record*, because nothing ever happened in Marston without him being the first to hear about it. When I swung open the door that day he was waiting. He turned and called a cheerful greeting. I had hardly given my order before he leaned across from the neighboring table and said in what was intended for a confidential voice, "So your pal Wright's solved the great problem."

I looked at him as if I didn't know what he was talking about. "My friend, Wright?"

"Well, isn't he a pal of yours?"

"I've only spoken to him about once."

"I thought he was visiting you the other night."

"He dropped in for a minute. Had a spot of evidence he thought might be useful in a case in which I'm interested."

"The lovely lady in the prison cell. You don't have to tell me, old boy, I know. Well, well. So he was interested too, was he? The dog!"

I was still trying to find adequate words for a retort when he went on, "I always think when a chap gets to that age and isn't married there's something fishy. What did he come to say?" He patted the chair beside him and I accepted the invitation.

"Just that he'd heard I was interested. He'd been away, you know."

"I know. Operation. That's why."

"Why what?"

"He shot himself."

"Because of the operation?"

"Because he wasn't cured and never could be. He couldn't stand the idea of being a chronic invalid."

"Look here," said I, "let's get this straight. You say Wright's dead?"

"That's it. As a door-nail."

"He did it himself?"

"He did."

"When was this?"

"He was found this morning. One of the servants. Police are swarming all over the place. You know, they'll ask for a rise of salary soon if they have so much to do."

I ignored that. "Well," I said, "I'm sorry and all that, but I didn't really know him. I suppose there'll be an inquest."

"Sure to be. You know, I'm beginning to think the Avenue is a place not to live. First Ross, then Wright—"

"Did Wright live in the Avenue? Yes, of course he did. It's a rotten thought, isn't it?"

"What's rotten?"

"That when you and I were asleep or mixing a last drink that poor devil was putting an end to himself."

"Anyone could tell you were a novelist," said Powis indulgently. "Anyhow, he's done for himself. Bad luck."

I couldn't eat; the food seemed to turn into lumps of leather in my mouth. I couldn't even swallow it; I sat there choking and staring.

"Apparently he left a three-volume novel explaining why he'd done it. I'm sorry for the poor devil that has to go through that. He had handwriting like a hen's tracks. Oh, well, it's a safe bet that verdict."

"The usual thing, I suppose. Suicide while of unsound mind."

"Had he any children?" I asked idly. Not that I cared.

"Keep it clean, old boy, keep it clean. He was a bachelor."

"Oh? Yes, I suppose so. I didn't know the fellow, you know. I suppose the servant found him."

"Yes. He'd been away for the night visiting a brother in hospital and when he came in he started tidying the house and when he opened the library door he got the shock of his life. And no wonder. I've seen a chap that shot himself and it isn't pretty—no, take my word for it, it isn't pretty."

I wondered how I was acquitting myself. The fact that Powis seemed to notice nothing wasn't much to go by. He was always too much obsessed by his own speech to pay much attention to his companion.

"When's the inquest?" I asked.

"Tomorrow morning, I believe. Hyde had a golf match on this afternoon and I suppose he didn't see why he should put it off. 'Tisn't as if he could help Wright now."

I wished the inquest might have been that afternoon. I wanted to hear the verdict, to know that nothing was suspected about the diary. Powis hadn't mentioned that, and I couldn't ask him.

I went back to my flat and thought hard. Wright's death couldn't have come at a better time from my point of view. I didn't know, of course, whether he had spoken about Viola Ross's mysterious visitor to anyone else. I couldn't afford to be too casual. Once the police became suspicious all the fat might be in the fire. But since it was known to Powis that the fellow had been to see me, it seemed quite probable that it would be known to other people too. I might be asked what he had come for. Since I had never, so far as my recollection went, spoken to Wright before it obviously could not be a casual friendly visit. He had only just come back to the place from a prolonged convalescence, and one of the first things he had done had been to call on a man he didn't know. A lot of people would ask the reason why. I remembered another of Crook's bits of advice.

It would be better to admit that he had come about Mrs. Ross, but I could shift the facts a little. To tell the truth spelled ruin, but if I said that he had been awake and had heard a man come up the path earlier in the evening, that might arouse just that amount of suspicion we needed to get Mrs. Ross acquitted. I thought about this so long that I didn't hear my telephone until it had rung several times. It was Sergeant Fisher at the other end.

"Will you be in for a short time, sir? There's just a statement we'd like to get in connection with Mr. Wright. You'll have heard about his death."

"I've just seen Mr. Powis," I said.

"Yes, sir. Well, we understand Mr. Wright came to see you the night before."

"Not to tell me he was proposing to commit suicide. I understand from Powis that it *is* suicide."

"That'll be for the coroner's jury to say, sir. But we have to get everything shipshape."

He meant that he was coming around to take my statement. I prepared myself to be as calm as possible. When he arrived I was at work.

"Sorry to interrupt you, sir, but we have to take all the evidence we can get as a matter of form. Now, about this visit . . ."

"I was pretty well surprised myself, because I didn't know the man. I supposed it must be urgent."

"And was it?"

"As a matter of fact, it was of primary importance. I suppose he didn't come to see you about it."

"No, sir."

"But he wrote or something? Oh, he must have done." I got up in considerable agitation. "Damn it all, Sergeant, he couldn't have been such a swine as to go without leaving a word."

"We had no communication of any sort from him."

I stood staring. "Well, I'm damned," I said.

"Why, sir?"

I sat on the edge of the table. "I'll tell you. You know I was on the Ross jury?"

"Yes, sir."

"And I wasn't satisfied that the evidence convicted Mrs. Ross. I wanted to be more certain. It's a pretty responsible job, sending a woman to be hanged. Wright had been away ever since Mr. Ross died. He got back and heard the stories going about—well, we don't have so many murders here that we can afford to treat them nonchalantly—and he came in to say that he had a bit of evidence to produce. He had been very wakeful that night, what with going to the hospital next day, the operation and all the rest of it—and he had heard the gate clang about ten-thirty. He had been in bed and he lifted the curtain and looked out. He saw a fellow go up the path. The light wasn't good enough for him to see who it was, but he banged on the door. He didn't get in, though, and a minute or two later he came back and slammed the gate. Wright said he slammed that gate as though he'd like to take it off its hinges."

Fisher looked puzzled. "Well, sir?"

"Doesn't that seem important to you?"

"Since he didn't get in . . ."

"He didn't get in by the front door. But there's a side door and a garden door. And if you come down at that hour to see a man it's generally pretty serious."

"Yes, sir." Fisher stroked his jaw. "You say he had no idea who he was?"

"He didn't see his face. He mightn't have recognized it if he had. But he told me he was coming to see you to make a statement."

"He didn't come."

"Why did he shoot himself?"

"He left a letter."

"So wrought up about his own affairs he couldn't think of anyone else, I suppose. If he'd written to you and posted it. . . ."

"We should have had it by now. I dare say he didn't give the matter another thought."

"And as he's dead the evidence can't be taken?"

"I'm afraid not, sir."

I walked across to the window. "It would have helped."

"I'm sorry, sir. He didn't say anything about himself?"

"Only that he'd had this operation and had just got back and was going to see his doctor."

"He told you that?"

"Yes, he told me that. He seemed pretty cheerful. I don't think he had the idea of suicide in his mind."

Fisher wasn't giving anything away. He got up and said he was sorry he had troubled me. It would be as well if I attended the inquest, just in case.

After he had gone I wondered exactly how the land lay. If Wright's evidence couldn't be taken I was no better off than before. All the same, I could spread the story. Then I remembered I had told Harry Ross the truth and decided Crook was undoubtedly right when he said you need to be intelligent above the average and to have the memory of a Recording Angel to be a successful liar.

I went to the inquest. A number of the local people turned up, but Wright hadn't been a popular fellow and everyone anticipated suicide, so there was no uncomfortable crowding.

His confidential man, Butler, was the first witness. He identified the body—there didn't appear to be any relations—and told his story. He had received an S.O.S. that morning relating to a brother who had been operated on for a ruptured appendix, and had received his employer's permission to spend the night away.

"What time did you leave?"

"At four o'clock sir. Mr. Wright said he would be dining out."

"So that at midnight he would be alone in the house?"

"Yes, sir. I did ask him if he was sure it would be all right, seeing he had been ill, and the houses on both sides were unoccupied, but he said he was, and I was to be back by mid-day the next day."

"Well?"

"I came back on time, but I was surprised to find the blinds had not been drawn. Mr. Wright is a very careful man, and doesn't like things to look wrong."

"You think he'd have drawn the blinds and curtains himself?"

"Not that, sir, but he was an early riser, and the young woman had been told to come in time to get his breakfast."

"Actually, she didn't turn up?"

"She says she came and she rang back and front but could get no reply. She assumed that Mr. Wright was sleeping."

"She didn't raise the alarm?"

"She went back to her home and said she couldn't get in. Then the postman called with a parcel and he could get no reply. He put the parcel on the step, and it was there when I arrived at about eleven o'clock."

"How did you get in?"

"I have a key to the back door, sir."

"Isn't that kept bolted?"

"No, sir. There is a Yale lock. I got in and began to get the house opened at once. That is, I drew the curtains in the dining and breakfast rooms, and having put on a kettle to boil, went up to see whether Mr. Wright was ready for breakfast. To my surprise I found the bed had not been slept in."

"And that alarmed you?"

"Not particularly, sir. I supposed that Mr. Wright must have changed his mind and gone to an hotel."

"When were your suspicions aroused?"

"When I went into the library. The curtains were drawn here but some light came between them."

"Yes, yes," said Hyde impatiently.

"When I opened the door I saw him there, and I knew that it was too late."

"Did you realize he was dead?"

"I saw the gun beside him, and I knelt down and touched him and he was cold. The room was in good order except for this. I telephoned to a doctor, saying that Mr. Wright had met with an accident."

"Did you think it was an accident?"

"It wasn't for me to think anything else, sir."

"And the doctor came?"

"Yes, sir. Dr. Forman that was. Dr. Renfrew was away. He'd been called to London for a consultation. It was Dr. Forman that Mr. Wright had seen that day."

"I see. Now, one more question. Of course, you saw Mr. Wright after he had seen the doctor?"

"Yes, sir."

"Did he seem at all put out? Upset? Strange in any way?"

"I can't say that he did, sir. Of course, if I'd have thought there was anything wrong I'd never have gone. . . ."

"I see."

Then Forman took the stand. He was an aggressive young man with a bush of flaming red hair. He agreed that he had seen Wright, that Wright had asked for the truth about his health and that he had told him.

"You think that was a judicious thing to have done?"

"He was neither a child nor an imbecile and I didn't feel justified in treating him as either. He asked for facts that must have come to his knowledge quite shortly."

"How did he take the information?"

"He was rather upset, not at the news so much as the fact that it must have been obvious to the doctors from the start that his was an incurable case."

"You didn't get the impression that he intended to do anything desperate?"

"Certainly not."

"If you hadn't told him the facts—he had no suspicion of them?"

"Er—no, I think not. He said, 'Tell me the truth. I'm better but am I cured?' What could I say?"

"What did you say?"

"I said, temporarily."

"You told him that?"

"Yes."

They didn't read the whole of Wright's letter to the court. Hyde said that it proved beyond all doubt that he had intended to take his own life, and gave a reason that many would consider adequate. The diary, kept meticulously, would show that he took an exaggerated interest in his own symptoms; a man with such a morbid interest was probably inclined to overbalance if he received a shock and such a shock he unquestionably had received.

Questions were asked about the revolver; it appeared that he had had it for some time, ever since a tramp scare in the neighborhood.

"There is actually a record in his diary as to when he bought it and why," said Hyde. "He noted every detail in his diary. It covers a good many years and was written almost up to the day of his death."

Butler here created a small sensation by rising in the court and saying, "Pardon me, sir, but did you say he wrote it on the night he shot himself?"

"No, not that night or the night before. But up till then."

"If you'll excuse me, sir, that's wrong."

"What do you mean, wrong?"

"Mr. Wright would make a note in his diary just as soon as a thing happened. I mean he wouldn't wait till the evening. That last day, I remember he did make a note. Some shares he held had gone down in value, and he always noted things like that."

"You mean he actually made a note the last day of his life?"

"Yes, sir. Before he went to see the doctor. I had come in to bring him his morning post—the mid-morning post, that is—and he was writing then."

"You're sure it was the diary?"

"Quite sure, sir."

"That's very strange. There's no entry after Monday night. Today is Thursday."

"You mean, there wasn't anything for Tuesday or Wednesday. Then, if you'll excuse me saying so, sir, somebody's been tampering with the book."

"What do you mean by that?"

"I mean, sir, that on Tuesday night Mr. Wright rang for me and asked me to bring him a fresh bottle of ink. He didn't write with a fountain pen, not ever, but with a quill. I brought him a new bottle and he said, 'Remember to order another one tomorrow.' I remember that quite well."

"There's something very strange here," said Hyde sharply. "There is no record of Tuesday or Wednesday." Fisher was in the court and he summoned him.

"I want to see that diary. Have you got it?"

"I'll bring it, sir."

I was hanging onto the chair in front of me. I

hadn't foreseen this. Even if anyone commented on the absence of entries on the Tuesday night it hadn't occurred to me that there would be any proof. I felt my forehead and hands were clammy with sweat.

Hyde was saying, "Do you think a page can have been abstracted here?" and both men bent over the book. The foreman of the jury was called, and then the book was passed to the other six jurors. The general view was that a page had been abstracted.

"We could prove that, sir," said Fisher calmly. "The book was bought locally." Hyde lifted his head; his face was white and his eyes like stones. In an instant the court was hushed, staring aghast. "What I was going to say, sir, was that we could get a duplicate and count the sheets. All these books are made to measure. But the way the string's been stretched just here, that looks as if a page had been taken out."

"You'd better get on with it," said Hyde. "That may make a difference to your verdict," he added to the jury.

"There's the letter, sir," said the foreman. "You aren't suggesting that anybody forged that."

"He's wasting his time in Marston if he did. He must be a master hand. It's difficult enough to read Wright's hand without having to copy it. Besides, who knew what the doctor had told him? And some of these facts—they couldn't have been set down by anyone but himself. No, no, I think we may take it that he took his own life."

Bagshaw, the police surgeon, intervened stiffly. "The weapon was held some inches from the face, instead of being pressed up against the temple as is usual in these cases."

The court was electrified. They hadn't anticipated the possibility of a second murder. Butler was recalled. He said there was no trace of any abstracted sheet in the room when he returned.

"Still, that doesn't mean that Mr. Wright didn't tear out the sheets himself and burn them. It's the most natural explanation."

A moment's thought convinced everyone that it was. The excitement began to die down; but that fool Butler started another hare.

"Excuse me for mentioning it, sir, but there is one point."

"What's that?"

"While I was waiting for the police I had a chance to look round, without touching anything, and I saw little bits of broken twigs and leaves on the floor."

"Well?"

"Well, sir, how did they get there?"

"What do you mean?"

"Leaves and twigs, sir."

"I suppose Mr. Wright brought them in on his coat."

"But how, sir? He hadn't been walking through a shrubbery. Besides, he always changed his coat when he came in, and he wouldn't be bringing leaves and twigs with him in any case."

The case was intolerably prolonged. Sitting speechless in my corner I found myself praying inarticulately for some sort of respite. It would be a classic absurdity if now they tried to involve me in this affair of his death. I was thankful I hadn't yielded to the momentary temptation to destroy the letter. No one could have forged such a hand. I began to see that by destroying the final entry I might have achieved definite harm. Yet how could I have left it in? It would have sealed Viola Ross's death warrant.

Hyde stopped all the speculation after a little. He told the jury it was their job to arrive at a conclusion. They only had to consider relevant facts. They had Wright's confession written in his inimitable hand; they had the fact that the revolver used was undoubtedly his; they had the doctor's evidence; against these there were a few leaves and twigs for which no one could absolutely account, but that might quite well have been brought in by the dead man. The most serious thing was Butler's evidence about the diary, but even if that had been tampered with, that didn't actually affect the verdict.

The jury retired. They were absent rather a long time, but eventually and without looking very happy about it they brought in a verdict of suicide while of unsound mind. The foreman then said they would like to add a rider. Hyde looked up suspiciously.

"Well?" he said in a sharp tone.

"We feel that further investigation should be made—"

Hyde nipped that in the bud. "You mean you're not satisfied as to the cause of death?"

"Oh, yes, we're quite satisfied that Mr. Wright took his own life, but we feel there's some evidence to be cleared up—"

"You're only here to decide the manner of the deceased's death. Anything else is outside your province."

The foreman sat down, crushed and indignant. The court emptied. Hyde caught my eye and nodded toward me. I made my way over to him.

"Look here, Arnold, I stopped that chap's mouth pretty brutally because I don't want more trouble than we can help. But I agree with him. There's more in this than meets the eye."

"You mean the twigs?"

"Why was the diary tampered with? It was, you know."

"You don't think he may have destroyed the sheets himself?"

"There's more to it than the destroyed sheets. I don't like that candle burning. The question is, what could he have got in that diary that someone didn't dare allow to become public?"

I said, staggered, "You're not suggesting blackmail?"

"Good Lord, no. But something is rotten in the state of Denmark. I'd like to know what it is. However, thank the stars that's not my job. I only have to discover, with the aid of the jury, how Wright died."

"Will the police keep on with the inquiry?"

"You'd better ask Fisher. I shouldn't be surprised. By the way, I hear Wright came to see you the night before."

"Yes. Had some evidence in the Ross case. Told me he was going to the police, and then he gets his own death sentence, and forgets other people have lives that are of importance to themselves, and does nothing about it."

"Do you seriously think it would have helped Mrs. Ross?"

"Might have raised that fraction of doubt that makes all the difference between the black cap and an acquittal."

THIRTEEN

UNHAPPILY, Fisher wasn't of the same mind. He went around sniffing out mysteries, discovered the broken twigs outside the window, concluded that a snapped end in the room fitted a certain branch and got to work as happily as a terrier digging out a rabbit-hole. Meanwhile I wasn't being left alone. The night after the inquest a reporter from the *Gazette* called to see me. He said he understood that Wright had been to see me on the day before his death. The press naturally was interested in Wright.

I was naturally anxious to make the most of this opportunity. As time went on I was becoming increasingly anxious on Mrs. Ross's behalf; I had, like Shakespeare's hapless hero, gone here and there and made myself a motley to the view, but actually I had accomplished very little.

I gave the reporter an interview, agreed that I had seen the dead man and repeated to him the story I had by this time told so often that I was beginning to believe it myself. The reporter being like the elephant's child, a creature of singular wit and sagacity, saw at once what a fine headline this would make. The Ross case was still very much in the public mind; most people believed Viola Ross guilty, but there were some prepared to give her the benefit of the doubt, and the usual percentage of people who detested the death sentence no matter how flagrant the offense.

"Who was this chap? No one knows?"

"No. It's a point, though, that he didn't come forward."

"Perhaps he was afraid he might be roped in."

"Must have had some guilty secret, then. After all, you don't go out and murder for fun." I could see his enthusiasm shining in his face.

"Who might have wanted the old boy out of the way besides the wife? What about the son?"

"There's no evidence against him at present, or at least none that has been offered."

"Wonder what he was doing the night Poppa died." I shrugged my shoulders to intimate that that was no concern of mine.

"Didn't the police get onto him?"

"Asked him about possible enemies, I believe."

"He wasn't on speaking terms with his father at the time, was he? Well, well, well. You can often not be on speaking terms but be on murdering terms."

I said dryly, "You'll remember the libel law, won't you?"

"My editor will, if I don't."

I didn't ask him his plans. I let him go and rang up Crook.

"H'm," said Crook characteristically. "Who was the fellow whom nothing in his life so became as his leaving of it? One of the Stuarts, wasn't it? Probably the first time our friend Wright has had an affinity with royalty. Pity about the diary, though. He may have had a note in it. Look here," his voice was stern, "you keep out of this for the next few days. Go duck-shooting on the Caspian or enter a monastery or get locked up for being drunk and disorderly, but for the Lord's sake let me handle this." I didn't tell him anything about the reporter. I didn't care how many people started making trouble. They couldn't very well make matters worse. I had the beginnings of a case against Ross.

The next thing that happened was the precipitate arrival of young Ross himself. He came in about cocktail hour the next day. He was perplexed, anxious, afraid and, on the surface at all events, angry.

"Look here," he began, "did you send that reporter fellow to me?"

"Certainly not. A man from the *Gazette* came here, seems to think he's going to solve all manner of mysteries."

"I've nothing to do with Wright's death."

"Nor have I, for that matter."

"He came to see you the night before he shot himself."

"That doesn't make me responsible."

"Who's trying to make you responsible? What I want to know is—why did you lie to me?"

"Lie?"

"Yes. Don't pretend. It's too late for that now. Why did you tell me that Wright had said he heard a man leaving the house at eleven-thirty when you knew damn well he said he saw a man trying to get in at half-past ten? Oh, you told that reporter the truth all right—" He broke off. I was staring.

"So you were there," I muttered. An instant later I saw the folly of that. He sprang to his feet.

"You're double-crossing me, and I want to know why. You're ready to do anything to try and get Viola off. It's become an obsession with you. I suppose you can't stand the thought that you might fail."

I said steadily, "Why didn't you say you were trying to get into your father's house that night?"

"You damned fool, what do you suppose people would have believed if I had?"

"That you were guilty."

"Obviously. And I wasn't."

"Did you tell this reporter that you were there?"

"Of course I didn't. I knew nothing. It's much the best."

I didn't speak, and he went on violently, "Look here, let's come to an understanding. You don't care who hangs so long as it isn't your candidate. It's the worst case of pride complex I've ever come across. I don't believe you even mind if she did kill him."

"We're wasting time," said I.

"What do you mean? Have you hidden someone behind the curtains? The police? Well?"

"Of course not. Don't be so melodramatic. I didn't even know you were coming down."

"But now you're going to them. Aren't you?"

"I don't know what I'm going to do," I replied candidly. "As you say, my one idea is to get Mrs. Ross acquitted, but that doesn't mean I want an innocent man put in her place. Only—you do agree that someone murdered your father?"

"It wasn't I," he exclaimed in a loud voice.

"No one says it was. But—"

He interrupted me. "If you don't think so, why are you making so much of the fact that I happened to be there? That fellow—Wright—told you I couldn't get in."

We didn't get much further. I could not, at that stage, tell him what was in my mind. I was adding them all up—the cigarette in the summerhouse, the revolver, the needle, the open window, the leaking heater—and wondering how much precisely they would amount to in a court of law. There was precious little actual proof. I wanted something more definite if I could find a way of getting it. The police, despite stringent inquiries, had not traced the gun or its owner. They had gone through the district with a tooth-comb, as they said, but though they had examined every fire-arms license and asked questions in every direction the affair remained unsolved. And now, I thought, I was once more in danger.

"I suppose," Ross said in a bitter voice, "you're in with that damned woman."

"What woman?" I was startled at his words.

"Oh, don't play the innocent with me. It's too late for that. I mean Irene Cobb."

"Irene Cobb? Why, I haven't seen her—but once—since your father's death."

"That so? Then, of course, you didn't know she'd got a job with Mrs. Judges."

"With Mrs. Judges?"

"That's what I said. Good God, man, don't repeat everything after me like a parrot."

"But Mrs. Judges? The thing's ludicrous. What kind of a job?"

"Ever hear Mrs. J. talk about the girl?"

"Well?"

"That's Irene Cobb."

I remembered in a flash—the girl who thought she was a lady, who had been a clerk, who had, according to Mrs. Judges, been "in trouble." So that's who she was. Irene Cobb. She had gone up, of course, to keep an eye on the pair of us, Ross and myself, but particularly, I thought, on me. Hers was one of those pitiable cases of frustration without an atom of harm or pathos to gild it. She was an unattractive creature and Teddy Ross was no more the Galahad of her dreams than she was a knight's lady. Her feeling for him had been morbid and overwhelming. Of that I was convinced. She had been furious when she realized that I was resolved to exculpate the widow. And then I recalled something else. And that was the picture of a figure in rather sketchy uniform disappearing out of the bathroom after young Ross had left it and before I myself had entered it. Had anyone else seen her? I didn't know. And supposing I told my story to the police now, in the light of this new knowledge?

I cursed fruitlessly in my heart. It wouldn't, of course, be proof that he had had nothing to do with the rag in the pipe, but it would provide the necessary element of doubt that is almost as valuable. Even the letters hadn't got the same significance as before, and it was upon these that I was founding my case against the dead man's son. Any counsel of intelligence—even a tyro like myself—would point out in Ross's defense that his room was open all day, that he himself was mostly out, and that it would be simple for a girl who worked in the house from dawn till dark to slip in for a minute, insert a sheet in the typewriter—hadn't she been a secretary? Oh! I could have ground my teeth with rage.

The window, of course, would be dismissed as a mere accident. There was no proof there. I had always recognized that. As for the needle—wouldn't authority argue that it was a woman's weapon rather than a man's, and hadn't she every opportunity for entering my room? The revolver? I could no more trace this to Harry Ross than I could to Irene Cobb, and the police had significantly failed to trace it to either.

I stood thinking fast. I had to take one more risk and I knew it. The devil of it was I couldn't be sure exactly what the risk would be. He must have one more chance of putting me out, and I had to create his opportunity for him.

My tongue felt like leather. I poured out a stiff drink of whiskey and soda and offered it to Ross, but he wouldn't touch it.

"Well," said I, lifting the glass to my lips.

The telephone bell rang. Mechanically I lowered the glass, took down the receiver. It was Bunty. I looked expectantly at Ross, but he didn't offer to move.

"Just a moment," I said. "I'll take this in the other room. Excuse me."

I went through into my bedroom, shutting the door firmly behind me. Bunty was in a new mood, a kind of chill anger in her voice.

"Richard, for the last time, I want to ask you to give all this up."

"My dearest! How can I?" I expostulated.

"Because *I* ask you to. Because I can't bear it any longer, the suspense, the misery. Because it isn't reasonable for you to go risking your life any longer."

"We've been over all this before," I said helplessly. "It isn't a matter of reason——"

"I know that. It's a matter of sheer crass obstinacy. Of stubborn pride. You won't give up now, because you're afraid of being laughed at, being pointed at as the man who lost his case. . . ."

"Bunty!" I cried.

But she swept on. "It's true. Well then, here's my ultimatum. Either you give it up, or you give me up. Whichever you please."

"This is insane," I cried. "You can't mean that."

"I do," said Bunty with finality. "Well?"

"I can't," I began again.

I heard the click as Bunty rang off without another word. I stood for a minute staring helplessly at the instrument. Oh, it was absurd, it was unfair. The sight of Ross erect and grim by the door brought me back to a sense of the instant's danger. What plot to destroy can a man lay in something under five minutes? I wondered as I shot lightning glances to left and right. Everything looked precisely as it had five minutes earlier.

"I'm going," Ross flung at me curtly. "I thought I'd just let you know I'm wise to your intrigue. I should be careful if I were you."

It was natural, even remembering the situation existing between us, for me to help him on with his coat, open the door, go with him into the hall. He was in a furious mood, jerked away when I offered him my hand, stamped out into the street. I came back into my room and closed the door. I sat down and buried my head in my hands. I had to think; I had to think clearly and swiftly, and all my thoughts were racing about in my head like blown leaves. "Tonight," I muttered to myself, "the last attempt will be made. And what will it be?"

A new thought occurred to me. At least I could write out a skeleton of my suspicions, of the incidents that had occurred, something that in an emergency would be discovered.

I drew out a fountain pen and unscrewed it.

I write this in case of emergencies, I began. *I have reason to believe that I am in great danger, and I cannot say how it will all end.*

I proceeded to detail my view of the position, the information I had obtained, everything that might point to Ross. I attached the two typewritten specimens to the page. I said nothing about Irene Cobb. I had no desire to distract attention from the main thesis. In any case nothing that happened tonight could be concerned with her.

When I had finished writing I signed the document and put it in the pocket of my overcoat. If the police ever had cause to examine my flat they'd find it there. Then I remained in my room with the light up and the curtains drawn. I didn't think I'd go to bed that night. Chill was spreading through my limbs. I looked at my watch. It was nearly two o'clock. I put out my hand and took up my almost untouched glass of whiskey and drained it in a couple of gulps.

The cold seemed to increase. I was shivering violently. It had attacked my vitals; I felt myself doubling with pain. I stood up, but I crumpled again almost immediately. It was no good. I stared around me. The pain was getting momentarily worse. My eye fell on the whiskey glass, in which only a dreg remained.

"The whiskey was poisoned," I shouted, as though the whole world could hear me. Then I collapsed on the carpet and writhed impotently in my anguish.

I am normally a very healthy man. I don't require the aid of doctors and at this critical moment I knew none personally.

I was by this time feeling so ill that I began to wonder whether I should die there on the floor. I groped my way with difficulty into the hall, crawled to the front door, and managed to get it open. No one was in sight, but as I hung there, half propped against the door, I heard the sound of footsteps very clear through the silence. I gave a feeble sort of cry; it sounded like a new-born kitten. The constable hove into sight.

At first, I think, he took it for a case of common drunkenness. He was a new man and not inclined to be sympathetic. He stooped down and gave me an arm; he wasn't particularly gentle about it.

"Look out, you fool," I said. "I'm poisoned."

"If you will drink cheap stuff," he began.

"It's what was in it," said I, and felt a further collapse was imminent.

"Get a doctor," I muttered.

I think that aroused him. "Where do you live?"

"In these flats. You can phone."

He became suddenly very alert and helpful. I fancy he saw himself getting promotion next week. He got me into my bedroom and took off my boots and covered me up. Then he took up the phone.

"I'll get Dr. Lawson. He doesn't make such a song and dance about coming out at night as most." Lawson proved to be a young man energetic and defensively unsympathetic. He was the kind that develops into the prominent specialist who doesn't need to mind his manners because he's got something better to offer and knows it.

"Well," said Lawson, when the constable opened the door—I could hear the conversation plainly—"what is it?"

"I found the fellow lying in the road—"

"Street accident? On my Sam, let 'em all die. Why

should I care? I'm only surprised there are any able-bodied people left in this town at all, seeing the way people speed. He's not one of my patients, is he?"

"He doesn't have doctors."

I could hear Lawson snort as he flung his coat across a chair. "He's glad enough to have one now. What's really the matter?"

"I told you, he was sort of propped against the door—"

"Why didn't you chuck a pail of water over him? That's the best cure—and the cheapest. I know these fellows. They're sick all over your best suit and then too drunk to recognize you when they're sober."

He came in, a tall, dark, powerfully built man.

"Well?" he said.

I muttered something about being poisoned.

He stooped his head. "Whiskey! I thought as much."

"That's it," said I.

The policeman looked up like a dog on scent. "Poisoned, did you say?"

"Why these chaps can't make a proper job of it I don't know," grumbled Lawson. "What did you take?"

It was difficult to persuade him this wasn't an affair of suicide. He took the glass the constable offered him, sniffed it, frowned, said something about an analysis. Then he turned back to me.

"May as well have you at the inquiry," he remarked. I suppose he administered some sort of antidote, but by that time I was beyond knowing or caring what was happening.

FOURTEEN

THE first visitor I had when the effects of the poison had begun to wear off was Fisher. I was still in bed when he arrived, looking remarkably official and armed with a notebook. I had been warned of his coming and I imagined he was going to ask questions about the whisky. For, of course, it had been doctored. I had known that before they told me that traces of poison were found in the dregs in the glass.

At first, I think, the doctor had suspected suicide. "You don't suppose I did it myself, do you?" I asked him.

"I'm not the police surgeon," returned he.

"Why the devil should I?"

"How the devil should I know?"

"I hadn't got any poison. Besides, it's absurd."

"Is it?"

I lay back after he had gone, thinking, "This is the most diabolical luck. I took this chance, and even now the stars in their courses seem to be fighting for young Ross."

When Fisher came in I supposed he wanted to discuss the circumstances. His expression was so grim that I began to think he shared Lawson's suspicions.

"Good morning, sir. Feeling better?"

"Thankful to be alive," said I.

"Yes, sir." He had about as much natural gaiety as an oyster. "A narrow squeak, I understand."

"Quite as narrow as I care about. What are the police doing about it?"

"That's what I came to see you about, sir."

"From your face, one might think you had a warrant in your pocket."

"According to the medical evidence, there was poison in the whisky you drank."

"Any reason to doubt the medical evidence?"

"None, sir. The question is—who put it there?"

"That's what I'd like to know."

"We shall find that out." He was as ponderous as an elephant.

"You haven't much choice," I pointed out.

"No, sir. Did you have any visitors that night?"

"Yes. Young Ross, the son of Edward, came to see me."

"Really, sir? About the new trial would that be?"

"About the Wright inquest."

I saw Fisher's brows lift. "Indeed! He hadn't any fresh evidence to offer?"

"I didn't know there was any doubt about that. What he came about was Wright's statement to me in connection with Edward Ross's death."

"Yes, sir?"

"He was the fellow Wright saw trying to get into the house."

I lay back expectantly. Fisher never moved a muscle. "He came to tell you that?"

"He did."

"It seems a long way to come to tell you that."

"He knew I was interested in the affair. It had seemed to me, as no doubt it had also seemed to you, that if we could show that someone was trying to get into the house on that evening, while Mrs. Ross was out, it would provide the possibility of an alternative criminal."

"Mr. Wright only said he tried to get in?"

"We've been over all this ground before," said I impatiently. "Of course, we can't prove anybody got in. I know that. But there was a chance—a British jury likes to be very sure of itself before it endorses the death penalty. Well, Harry Ross came down to tell me he was the man in question."

"I wonder why he did that."

"To dispel my false hopes, I suppose."

"It seems queer to me. If he hadn't spoken, you wouldn't have known, would you?"

"I knew he was in the neighborhood."

"But you didn't know he came to the house."

"No, of course I didn't."

"That's why I say it's queer he should tell you."

"Don't you see, he had to have some reason. Besides, he may have thought it was safe to tell me. Dead men tell no tales."

"You connect him with the poisoned whisky, sir?"

"Well, poison doesn't put itself into whisky."

"Quite so. You are making a charge against him?"

"Look here," I exploded, "what do you suppose I pay taxes for? Don't I get any police protection?"

"Do you require it?"

"I admit it hasn't helped me. It's no thanks to the police that I'm not dead."

"It isn't for us to prevent gentlemen putting poison into glasses. We don't come into a case until a crime's been committed."

"Are you still unconvinced that such a crime has been committed?"

"No, sir. But, naturally, we want to be sure of our facts."

"All this means you think I may have done it myself. But I assure you I'd have done the job properly, no half measures that result in my being three-quarters dead and then brought back to life to face a trial for attempted suicide. Besides, why the devil should I?"

"That's a point I came to discuss with you, sir. I'd like your statement."

"I don't think I've much to add. I've told you what happened. If you mean opportunity, he had that. I was crazy enough to leave the fellow alone with the whisky glass while I telephoned from another room . . . "

"I didn't mean that exactly. I'm coming to that. I meant in respect to this." He opened his hand, and showed me something small lying in the palm. I peered more closely.

"What's that?"

"A button."

"So it is. Why bring it to me?"

"It seems to fit one of your coats."

"One of mine? It's a very ordinary sort of button, isn't it?"

"The button by itself wouldn't mean anything, but there's this," and he indicated the strip of material adhering to it.

"Oh, I see. You mean, that ought to help you to trace the jacket it came off."

"Precisely, sir."

"And you've traced it?"

"There's a coat in your wardrobe, sir, with a button missing."

"And it all fits like a jigsaw puzzle?"

"That's right."

"Well?" I looked as perplexed as I felt. "What of it? Where did you find it?"

"In the bushes outside Mr. Wright's library window."

I was too staggered to speak. The events of the past day or two had driven the recollection of Wright and his suicide out of my mind.

"You'll remember Butler's evidence about the twigs and leaves on the carpet," the sergeant went on. "We made the necessary examination and we found this. We've been trying to trace it."

I still kept silent. I was in the soup all right now. There was nothing for it but to tell the facts. It would be useless to hedge. I cursed my own folly in not examining my coat after I left the house, but my one desire at that time had been to get away.

"How did you find it?" I asked presently.

"When you were unconscious you kept talking about a letter in a pocket, and we began to look for it . . . "

"And found that?"

"Yes, sir."

I drew a long breath. "I suppose I shall have to tell you the facts. It's true, I was there that night, though I had no hand in his death."

"No, sir?" Fisher, who had displayed a glimpse of humanity for an instant, resolved into the robot again.

"No. The fact is I was coming past the house when I heard the sound of a shot. It was about midnight and the place was very quiet. I mean, it couldn't have been a bursting motor tire or something of that kind, because there was no traffic in sight. The houses on either side of Wright's, as you know, are standing empty. There were no lights in the windows of his house, but I pushed open the gate and walked up the drive and hammered on the door. Nothing happened. I rang the bell and still nothing happened. I suppose the obvious thing would have been to ring you up, but I didn't know what had been going on; it might have been an accident, a man might have been badly injured; my one idea was to get into the house and find out what was wrong. I remembered that those houses can be approached from the back, so I turned out of Romary Road into Little David Lane, and went through the garden. There was a light at a ground floor window and I could look through the curtains. I could just make out a figure on the floor. The window was open and I opened it wider and squeezed my way in. Wright was lying where he was subsequently found and the gun was on the rug beside him. I could see at once that he was dead. Well, you saw the body yourself."

Fisher nodded. "Yes, sir. You didn't inform any-one?"

"No. I suppose I lost my head. All I wanted to do was to get out of that room. I couldn't do anything, the man was nothing to me, but I wanted to get away. I didn't even know why he'd taken his own life."

"You knew who he was?"

"No." I shuddered. "I didn't even realize that. He wasn't a man I had ever known; I had seen him once, and then that night—he might have been Adam dragged from the nettly grave. No one—no one could have recognized him."

Fisher displayed a little more of his human side. "I know, sir. Well, you didn't do anything?"

"No. I just scrambled out of the window again and came back. When I was home it did occur to me to telephone but . . . " I stopped.

"But you didn't."

"No. It sounded such a damned queer story and I suddenly remembered all the yarns I'd read about in-nocent men being arrested for murders they hadn't committed. It might have sounded strange, my breaking into the man's house by the back way—and I didn't even know who he was. I see now that I ought to have telephoned at once. There was a phone in the room, I remember. Perhaps if he hadn't looked so ghastly I should have done the right thing."

"He wasn't a friend of yours, you say?"

"I'd only seen him that once, as I told you before."

Fisher stroked his long jaw. "I see," he said.

"Do you?" I felt bitter. "Heaven knows how all this is going to end."

"Would you have any objection to signing a statement, sir, as to what you've just told me?"

"About going into Wright's room?"

"Yes, sir."

"I don't mind," I said. "Tell me one thing, though. Are they trying to upset the jury's verdict in the Wright case?"

"Oh, no. There's no doubt he committed suicide. Only it was difficult to understand about the pages in the diary being destroyed."

"It was an accident, I suppose. There was a candle burning on the table, I remember."

"Yes. There seems to have been. You didn't destroy the pages, sir?"

"I didn't touch the diary. I had no reason to want to. After all, it was all in my favor if Wright had made an entry about the man trying to get in at ten-thirty."

"Naturally, Mr. Arnold. That's why it seems so curious."

I didn't feel awfully happy after Fisher had gone. I knew I was as innocent of Wright's death as the man in the moon, but I cursed myself for allowing them to collect the proof that I had been in the room on that night. They couldn't make me say I had touched the diary and they couldn't unearth an atom of proof, but I was uneasy all the same. I wondered what they'd do about Harry Ross and the poison. Presumably I could bring a charge, but my conversations with the doctor

and with the police had made me realize that once again
I was in a blind alley. The situation seemed to me
to be becoming more and more desperate; and meanwhile there was Viola Ross in prison and I was no nearer
showing that she hadn't murdered her husband than
I had been at the outset. Presently I remembered the
letter I had written that night; Fisher hadn't referred
to it. I wondered whether he had found it.

I staggered out of bed and began to examine my
overcoat. At first I thought it had gone, then I felt
something crackle, and discovered that the envelope
had slipped between the coat and the lining. That's
another disadvantage of being your own valet. You
don't notice these things. I shoved the letter into
another envelope with a covering note.

"This is the document I kept referring to in my
delirium," I said. "It may be of interest to you."

Nothing happened for forty-eight hours. Then Fisher
came again, and brought a constable with him. I was
out of bed, though still rather shaky. I saw them in my
sitting room.

Fisher spoke at once. "Richard Oliver Arnold," he
said, "I have a warrant here for your arrest on a charge
of murdering Arthur Fielding by gas poisoning on June
the 29th. You need say nothing, but if you do make
any statement I have to warn you that anything you
say may be used against you."

There are some things so appalling that they are
not even conceivable, not as happening to oneself, that
is. They may appear as possibilities, remote but not

absolutely unthinkable, in connection with other people, but never, never as applied to oneself. I had sufficient wit to refuse to say anything until I had seen Crook. He, surely, would know how to deal with this absurd situation. It struck me as odd, even as sardonically entertaining that I, a free man, having undertaken the defense of a woman whom I claimed to be innocent of a capital offense, should end by being myself arrested on a similar charge. During the endless hours that intervened before Crook appeared I invented, bettered, perfected the speeches I would make when my chance came.

"Well, well," said he, "now perhaps you'll realize I know my onions when I warn you to keep off the legal turf. It's no use, old boy. I know that once in a hundred times an outsider romps home, but it ain't safe to back outsiders unless you know a damn' sight more about form than you do. No offense, of course, but if you'd gone duck shooting on the Caspian or something comparatively harmless like that you wouldn't find yourself in jug now."

"No," I agreed, with some bitterness, "and Viola Ross would have been hanged for murder, and everyone would have been satisfied."

"Well, anyhow, Fielding would be alive, and you also."

"I'm alive still and I propose to remain so. As for Fielding, there's already been an official verdict in his case."

"Ever hear of a beggar called Marcus Aurelius? When I was a kid an aunt of mine sent me his meditations or whatever they were called. Dinky little volume with a picture of an old gentleman in a violet coat, wearing a white topper, walking among lavender beds. Admittin' you were wrong is only the same thing as sayin' you're wiser today than you were yesterday. That's one of his sayings. Well, even the police don't mind admittin' now there's something to be said for the old boy that coined that."

"I suppose they're serious in their charge," said I.

"D'you know what a murder trial costs the country? Five thousand pounds. And that's not countin' your contribution. They don't run the community into that without stoppin' to think."

"But why on earth do they pick on me?" I demanded.

"Well, it could be, you know," allowed Crook.

"You mean I could have murdered him?"

"You were in the bathroom before he was."

"So was Ross. And what motive had I?"

"What motive had Ross?"

"He didn't know Fielding was going to be next. He thought it would be me."

"And put the towel in place?"

"It was one of a series of attempts to put me out."

"Endin' with the poison in the whisky?"

"Yes."

"And none of them successful?"

"None of them—unless you call the police's latest move successful."

"You'll get the benefit of the doubt," Crook encouraged me.

"But—but what about motive? I hadn't anything against old Fielding."

214

"You didn't know you were being called to be at the phone, did you?"

"Not at that moment."

"So you didn't know Fielding was going to be there, either?"

"Of course, I didn't. I hardly knew of the old man's existence."

"Well, then, don't you see?"

"I'm damned if I do."

"I'll tell you." His heavy features hardened. "I'm your lawyer. It's my job to do what I can for you. The best thing I can do at the minute is tell the truth. Mind you, I don't always say that's the best policy. There's a lot in what that chap, Anthony Hope, said, that truth's a valuable commodity, too damn' valuable to be wasted where it won't be appreciated, but only the truth's any good here, and that may not be much use. Just think back to all that's happened since Teddy Ross died. First of all, there's Mrs. Ross's arrest and trial."

"Yes."

"You stopped her being hanged out of hand."

"I didn't think she had done it."

"Quite, quite. I'm not questioning your motives, only that's the fact. Well, if she hadn't done it someone else had and you needed a substitute. There wasn't much choice, but young Ross seemed to fit the bill. He was going to be cut out of the will, he had to have money, he wasn't on good terms with Papa anyway. So he was fair game. You found out he was in that part of the world that night . . . "

"And at the house," I interrupted.

"You didn't know that. That was only speculation."

"He told me."

"When?"

"The night I was poisoned."

Crook eyed me reproachfully. "You're about six fields ahead of the hounds," he said. "You didn't know then. You just fixed on him as the most likely person to have done it, if Mrs. Ross didn't."

"Well, wasn't he?"

"Oh, yes." Crook sighed. "We'd earn our daily bread and treacle a lot easier if things happened that way. Well, as soon as you began to trail him things started happenin'. First of all, there was the window."

"I realize you can't bring that into court," said I, with some bitterness. "There isn't a scrap of proof. He only has to say my foot slipped, and he was trying to save me."

"Quite."

"I dare say he thought of that."

"Next," said Crook.

"The gun."

"How much proof have you got there?"

"None at all."

"That's what I thought. I say, how much did you tell that bobby?"

"I didn't say a thing. I was too much flabbergasted for one thing."

"I meant before that, when they were asking about the button?"

"I just answered his questions. I'd nothing to fear."

Crook's face seemed to swell till it resembled some monstrous caricature of Punch.

"Nothing to fear, old boy? When you'd been concealing facts from the police?"

"As an innocent man," I began, but he stopped me on the word.

"Don't play the ingenue here," he begged. "You know as well as I do that in spite of all the text books every man's guilty till he has been proved innocent—or acquitted anyway. Not in the eyes of the law perhaps, but in the mind of God Almighty's Bodyguard, the British Police Force, that's the first and the only truth that matters. So you told 'em about going into the room?"

"Yes. I couldn't very well deny it."

"No, but you might have staged a faint and not been able to discuss it till you'd seen me."

"Would they have let me see a lawyer?"

"Perhaps not, but your own doctor could have called. Every sick man has a right to see his doctor." One heavily veined lid dropped in a stupendous wink.

"Anyhow, they were bound to find out. And it isn't a crime."

"You could have given evidence at the inquest. You weren't involved."

"I didn't think they'd ever find out. There was nothing useful I could add. And there was all that stink about the diary."

"But you didn't know anything about the diary."

"Of course, I didn't. Not until the inquest."

"It'll strike a lot of chaps as queer that you didn't

217

say anything. Still, as you say, they can't hang you on that. Well, let's *revenons à nos moutons*. We've disposed of the window. You've admitted you can't bring the gun home to Ross. Where was he that night?"

"Officially at the dog races."

"Then that lets him out."

"Why? I don't suppose he can prove it."

"He doesn't have to. We've got to prove he wasn't and you tell me, my boy, how we're going to do that. If you could show he ever had a gun . . . "

"I suppose you could find out if he ever had a license . . . "

"He didn't. Don't try and teach me the preliminary steps."

"Still you can have a gun without a license, just like you can keep a dog."

"If you're lucky. But why should he have one? These London chaps don't need guns what with buses and trains and whatnot. Unless you think he bought it for the occasion."

"He might have done so."

"What the soldier said ain't evidence. Besides, it's a tricky way of doing a chap in. You've got to get down to the place, you've got to fix the gun, you've got to get into the other fellow's room somehow, you've got to risk being seen going or coming or being found on the premises, you've got to hang about till he shows up and he may not come that night at all, you've got to risk his only bein' wounded; you may be seen gettin' over the wall, some nosey parker may see you chucking the gun away, if you keep it it can be identified. Another thing—those letters."

"Letters?"

"Yes, the anonymous letters that were missing. Where did you keep 'em?"

"In a drawer in my room."

"Very careless, that," said Crook severely.

"I like that—from you," exclaimed I, stung into anger. "Haven't you always preached the gospel of putting things in obvious places!"

"So they shan't be found. No use putting them there if they are. These seem to have been found with remarkable ease."

I looked at him. "What does that mean?"

"They're gettin' Forbes to do the case for the Crown. That chap might not be able to get Judas Iscariot into Heaven, but anything short of that is child's play to him. And he'll make it look almighty strange that the fellow knew where to look at once."

"We don't know where he looked. He may have ransacked the place."

"He left it uncommonly tidy if he did. How did he know you hadn't handed them over already?"

"I suppose that was the chance he took."

"And then went on writin' letters. By the way, why to Miss Friar?"

"We were engaged."

"That's one for the press. They generally smell these things out like a dog tracking straight for the garbage pail."

"We'd deliberately kept it quiet. Her father didn't approve. He didn't think I had enough money."

"But she had enough for two, eh?"

"I didn't want to live on her money. I didn't need to."

"Spoken like a gentleman," approved Crook. "All the same, someone must have talked."

"I don't think so. No one breathed a word to me."

"Did she know young Ross?"

"I don't think she ever met him."

"Funny he knew about the engagement then."

"What makes you think he did?"

"Well, if not why write the letters to her? He might as well have written them to the man who kept the pub."

I was silent for a minute or two. "Then he must have known," I said, at last. "After all, a man who's trying to escape the gallows is going to be pretty careful. And I did go up and see her and she telephoned me . . ."

"He got wise very early in the game. Forbes'll make a lot of that. Well, what about the letter you did keep? Where is it now?"

"The police have it. Anyway that was typed on his machine."

"Did he keep his room locked?"

"No, none of us did in that house. I wouldn't have found the needle in my pillow if we had."

"Perhaps he kept the machine locked?"

"He couldn't. It only had a soft cover."

"You know that?"

"Rather. I went into his room to see him and the machine was on a table in the window."

"Forbes will make mincemeat of that. Was he there, by the way?"

"Yes."

"Could you have got into the room if he hadn't been?"

"Yes, I suppose so."

"And so could anyone else."

"They could. He got rid of the machine directly that other letter was typed."

"Men do buy new machines."

"It was a pretty odd coincidence."

"You meet coincidence everywhere except in novels. Novelists are such conceited chaps, they won't be grateful for coincidence. Everything's got to fit together, with a meaning. There ain't much meaning in life, dear boy. That's what you can't get 'em to understand."

"I realized some time ago the letters wouldn't help. I realized that when I heard about Irene Cobb being in the house."

"She being the late lamented's secretary?"

"That's the girl."

"And she might have taken a hand?"

"What was there to prevent it?"

"What was her motive?"

"She didn't want to see Viola Ross acquitted. She hated the woman."

"In love with Teddy?"

"Something of the kind. If it hadn't been for her no one would ever had questioned his death being anything but natural causes. She asked about the clock."

"The disadvantage of taking to murder is that it

gives you so little scope, unless you're lucky or cleverer than the average. If you go in for burglary you may get caught on the job, but by the time you come out of clink you've picked up a lot of useful hints for your next job. But the murderer don't get that chance. His first job is usually his last, and even if he's successful it's as much luck as anything. And as Scott Egerton always said, the last trump always lies with fate and she bein' female, there's no tellin' how she'll play it. Women have a way of goin' all moral on you when you least expect it. That's their danger. The most immoral woman will get indignant over another woman cheating London Transport of a penny fare. If this chap had had some experience he'd have remembered the clock; you can't expect a tyro to think of everything. Well, well, you can't do much with those letters. What comes after that?"

"The needle. I found a great carpet sharp in my pillow when I came back from the post."

Crook's great head nodded like an overblown peony, topheavy on its stalk. "I know. Nasty trick that. Needle breaks off in the essential vertebrae, probably below the surface, nobody finds it, death a mystery, another of these novelist chaps, always out for a sensation and a spot of limelight; serve him damn well right. Shovel him underground without waste of time. Only millionaires and Cabinet Ministers can afford that sort of death. For the rest of the world it's:

Rattle his bones over the stones,
He's only a pauper whom nobody owns.

"You know, either you're astonishingly unlucky or Ross has the luck of the damned. There isn't one of these chances that can be brought home to him. Forbes'll make a lot of that. You know, I'm almost sorry they didn't take him. I'd like to act for the fellow. I like a bold sinner. I can't stand your timid muddlers who give you a little push when the train's coming in— by the way, he didn't try that?"

"The only time I was travelling with him, I gave him no opportunity."

"It's when you're not travelling with him you want to watch out. What happened then?"

"The next thing was the bath incident, for which they have arrested me. Why they should imagine I wanted old Fielding murdered . . . "

"Nobody wanted old Fielding murdered, not Ross, not yourself, definitely not Fielding. Nobody knew it would be Fielding."

"Then I was trying to murder myself?"

"No, no. But you were trying to make it appear that Ross was trying to murder you. It all sounds a bit involved, but in reality it is perfectly straightforward."

"I'm glad you think so," said I, in bitter tones.

"Be logical," he reproved me. "You're a novelist, you've got some imagination. Put yourself in Forbes' place. He don't care if Mrs. Ross hangs or not; he don't care if you do. All he's paid for is to make out a case against you, just as I'm paid to get you out of this jail if I can. He's been given a lot of facts—the window, the letters, the needle, the gun, the bath. Your story is that Ross is responsible for the lot; his is that you are, and you know—it could be, it could be, Arnold. You could have tried to fake the window accident, it could be your gun as easily as his, you could have put the needle in the pillow, the cigarette in the summer-house and the rag in the pipe, and even the poison in the whisky."

I sat back shaking and appalled. "Is that the case they're trying to bring against me?"

"I don't know exactly because I haven't seen Forbes yet, but in his place it's what I'd be doing. There's no proof either way, but either Ross is a pretty heavy bungler or you're guarded by a very competent angel. It isn't every man that has five or six attempts made against his life, and comes up smiling every time. It's a pity," he added, "you can't produce the other letters. You see what Forbes will make of it?"

"No."

"You're tired," said Crook, tolerantly. "He'll say those letters were lost precisely because they weren't typed on Ross's machine."

"On whose, then?"

"You're a writer, ain't you?"

"A lot of people seem to have discovered that lately, who didn't know it before."

"And you'd have a typewriter?"

There was another silence while I digested that. "You mean, they'd say I wrote the original anonymous letters myself?"

"No proof, have you?"

"I haven't got to prove I didn't. They've got to prove

224

I did."

"They can't do that. But they'll throw it out as a suggestion. Now we come to . . . "

"The whisky," I interrupted. "Did I poison that and nearly kill myself?"

"The law don't like things being done by halves. If you'd gone the whole hog, died as a result of the nightcap, they'd feel much more kindly towards you."

"Where did I get the poison from?"

"Where did Ross? They haven't found any traces anywhere. It's still six of one and half a dozen of the other."

"Then why pick on me? Or do they toss for it?"

"Tut-tut, old boy. They ain't sportsmen, they're lawyers. Why you? Oh, the Wright affair, of course."

"But they aren't suggesting I murdered him?"

"No. They don't care a trouser button about him. But they're interested in his legacy."

"Which was that?"

"The diary. You see, it's as plain as the nose on my face, and that must be as plain as anything this side of the grave, that some fellow cut it about. They like a seasoning of logic, do the police, so they begin to ask why? Wright was going to polish himself off. Why should he burn the particular bit of his diary that referred to Mrs. Ross? Burn one bit and destroy without any trace the other? We know he'd made entries, and the entries had disappeared. And—I told you the lawyers don't object to coincidence but only as a dash, a soupcon to flavor a case. And there's been rather too much coincidence here. Their argument will be that some chap destroyed those pages because they were dangerous. Now, you can't argue that they were dangerous to young Ross."

"But they were," I insisted. "There was a record of his surreptitious visit."

"But without the name. Even if the whole world suspected him nobody could prove it. He only had to lie low, and he was safe enough. Besides, it's straining the position too far to suggest that on that particular night there were two of you hanging about Wright's house. You can't expect to have things handed to you with parsley around the dish every time."

"But that's exactly what I did anticipate," said I warmly. "I had told him of the entry."

"Why?"

"In the hope that he would give himself away."

"That's something I wanted to ask you about. Why did you pelt off to town to tell him?"

"I thought he might give himself away."

"And why did you tell him one story and the court another?"

"I don't understand you."

Crook leaned forward and put a hand like a ham on my knee. "See here, Arnold, I'm not the police. I ain't a judge, I ain't a neuter conception of justice. I'm just a yellow dog of a lawyer who's known more crooked folk than straight in his time. And I've got to have the truth if I'm to do anything to help you. You told young Ross half-past eleven . . . "

"I hoped the shock would make him speak, that he'd say, 'No, he's got it wrong, it was half-past ten when

I was there.' That might have let Mrs. Ross out."

"But he didn't say it?"

"No, not then."

"When did he?"

"When he came down here that night, after the inquest."

"He came to tell you he was there?"

"He came to ask why I'd told him half-past eleven."

"And why had you?"

"I've told you."

Crook shook his massive head. "That cock won't fight, old boy."

"What do you mean?"

"Forbes will offer the jury a better explanation than that."

"What will he say?"

"That the pages were obliterated or destroyed because the actual entry was half-past eleven. And he'll go further. He'll say they were obviously destroyed by the man who did leave The Laurels at eleven forty-five on the day of Teddy Ross's death. And he'll tell you why."

"What will he say?" I didn't know my own voice, so weak, variable was it.

"He'll say that the man who destroyed that record is the man who was Viola Ross's companion, the man who murdered Teddy Ross, the man who's been raising heaven and earth ever since to get Viola Ross acquitted."

After that the silence seemed to last forever. I don't know whether it took me a long time to accept the implications of that remark, or whether it simply was that, as in all times of acute crisis, time seemed focused to a single point, this instant of experience, so that one saw the world as from a bell of glass, perceiving outward events yet hearing nothing of their thunder, observing people passing yet seeing them only as shadows disconnected from any personal issue. At last I lifted my eyes. Crook's sturdy bulk seemed to fill the cell.

"You mean there will be a suggestion that *I* killed Teddy Ross?"

"More than a suggestion. There was no sense in the Fielding murder—or manslaughter if you like—I'm not the judge or the jury—unless it led on from some other crime. That's the devil of murder. Either you've got to shoot your bolt and be satisfied and chance it, or you must go on covering up your mistakes."

I said harshly, "They won't bring it home to me. The thing's absurd."

"More absurd than your counter-accusation against Ross?"

"Of course. He had motive enough, God knows. Ross thought he was making love to his wife; he was putting a detective onto her."

"No one knew that until after his death."

"Viola Ross did. He had told her that night."

"She didn't let that come out at the trial, did she?"

"Of course she didn't. She's not an absolute fool."

"Then—that's interesting, Arnold, that's damned interesting. I mean—you haven't seen her since she was arrested, have you?"

"No. I . . . "

He interrupted me. "I was wondering how the devil you knew that—unless of course, she told you."

"She . . . " I began, and then stopped. I saw the ambush into which I'd walked. Crook, naturally, saw it too.

"So she told you after Ross had told her and before he was killed. Quick work. Miss Cobb was right. She did go out to telephone to a lover—only the lover wasn't Harry Ross."

I said sharply, "I admit nothing."

"Quite right, old boy. It doesn't matter your having told me. I'm your lawyer. But look out you don't admit that in court. It spells ruin for you if you do. And Forbes is devilishly sly, so sly he's got your story out of you before you know you've begun to talk. It's a pity you can't be deaf and dumb for the benefit of the trial, but I suppose that would be asking too much."

"Then you assume that the police are right?"

"I'm a lawyer. Lawyers don't assume. It ain't their job. Journalists assume, even pressmen assume, but not lawyers."

After he had gone away I sat without moving for a long time. I could hear feet going past, feet always moving away from me. I thought that never again should I hear the welcome sound of feet coming towards me, except the feet of the men coming to take me to the court and presently coming to take me to the little shed that they whitewash afresh for 'every execution. I should be a piece of merchandise for which a receipt has to be given; I should cost the country approximately five thousand pounds, Crook had told me.

They'd have to buy two sacks of quicklime instead of flowers for my grave. It didn't bear thinking of.

I was defeated by bad luck, I told myself. I couldn't have allowed for Wright. Of course, I could have let him tell his story and leave it to the courts to discover the man. I could have done that, but I felt it was dangerous. You see, one person besides myself knew the truth and that person was Viola. I don't say she would have told it, but she wouldn't have allowed Harry to die on her account, and I couldn't let her die when I knew she was innocent. Because the other person who knew the truth was myself. Crook was right. I killed Teddy Ross, and if it weren't for all the trouble that has followed I shouldn't care a tinker's curse. I couldn't have foreseen this. I suppose every murderer says that.

The queer thing is that although two men have died, each of them without deliberation on my part, on account of acts of mine, I can't feel I'm a murderer. I didn't mean to murder Teddy, I certainly didn't mean to murder that old man. While I still have the chance I'm going to set down the facts and the court can do what it likes with them.

FIFTEEN

When I first met Viola Ross I thought what a fine mistress she would make. Not a wife—I never thought of her as a wife. There's a flavor of domesticity, a monotony, a permanence about a wife that her vitality, her secrecy, never suggested. I knew nothing about her except that she was married to a little rat of a man who had to be careful about his health. I don't think it ever occurred to me that she was faithful to him. We were lovers almost at once; she had a reckless streak in her, wouldn't have minded telling Teddy the truth, even smashing up the home. That wasn't my idea at all. We could have our fun without all that extravagance, I said. She agreed to everything. We were quite careful. We were never seen together in Marston; she had plenty of excuses for coming to town, and it was in town that we met. She was, as I expected, a perfect mistress. But Viola was like the rest; she couldn't treat the matter as an incident in which we could both delight, and presently pass on to the next adventure. She became difficult; spoke of her husband.

"If he finds out," she would say.

"He won't, if you exercise reasonable care. Besides,

you're not doing him any wrong. You told me there's been nothing between you for ages."

"There would be if he thought there was another man. He's like that."

Later she told me that he did suspect, that he was changing their domestic arrangements.

"Has he got me pinned down?" I asked.

"No, I believe he thinks it's Harry, just because I backed the boy against him. I was right, wasn't I? You believe I was right."

I didn't care what happened to Harry. I never have. I shouldn't have minded if he'd swung. I'd a good deal rather he had hanged than that I should.

"Let him go on thinking that," I suggested. "You can lend color to the situation by going on seeing him when you're in town."

She agreed again; whenever she came up—or at least pretty often—she would go and visit her stepson. Ross became madder and madder.

"One of these days he'll take a knife and cut my throat," said Viola to me.

"Not he. He wouldn't have the guts."

"I'm glad he hasn't a gun. He might use that."

I offered to end the situation; I was beginning to think a change of climate would be beneficial to us all. Viola was beginning to usurp those tiresome privileges that wives invariably assume. She would question me as to my movements, whom I had seen, where I had been, the identity of my companion. I resented the situation. If I chose to go out with another woman, that was my affair. Once or twice there were scenes; once

232

for a fortnight we held no communication. I meditated the wisdom of making a dash for it. I wanted to go to New York. But I knew Viola. She was perfectly capable of telling Teddy the truth and coming after me. I decided it would be better to handle the situation with velvet gloves. By this time the affair had ceased to be an adventure and had become a tie. I kept on wondering whether she had told Teddy, whether she was planning to let him find out.

About this time I met Bunty Friar. I suppose after I'm dead, people will say I simply wanted her for her money, but that wouldn't be true. I don't say I'd have given her a second thought if she had been a poor woman, but she's the only woman I've ever met to whom, I think, I could have stayed faithful. I wanted her fiercely, so fiercely that I began to hate Viola for being in my way. Why couldn't she end the affair gracefully? It had begun as an entertainment on the side. I had never wanted it to be anything more. All the same, I knew my danger. I couldn't announce my engagement to Bunty so long as Viola was in the offing.

Then matters got worse. Viola said she knew Teddy suspected.

"Suspects what?" said I.

"That I have a lover."

"Does he know it's me?"

"I don't think so. But if he asks me it may be difficult to deceive him."

I shall never know whether she gave the position away. She swears she did not, and that may be the truth. But on the day that he died he received a letter in which our names were linked. That evening she rang me up.

"I have just had the most terrible scene with Edward."

"What is it this time?"

"He has got a letter telling him about us. He says he will bring it into court."

"The devil he has. What's he going to do?"

"He's putting a detective onto us."

"We'd better be careful. It might be wise to go away for a bit."

"Both of us?"

"No, no. Don't be ridiculous. But if you're not meeting me there'll be nothing for the chap to find out."

"He is going to work backwards. It's too late to go away, unless we go together."

But that wasn't what I wanted at all. "You'd better sit tight and do nothing for the moment. Being seen together in London isn't a crime, and we've been much too careful in London to give any evidence to the other side."

"I must see you," she insisted. "I must see you tonight."

"But that's absurd. We can't . . . it wouldn't be safe."

"I have thought it all out. He will be busy with examination papers this evening; I shall go to the movies. I often go to the pictures. You also can come to the pictures, you understand, but if we leave towards the end we are not likely to be noticed."

If I had refused she would have come around to my

flat. I had to agree. We met all right and we talked. I don't think anyone saw us. In fact, I know they didn't or it would have come out long ago. It seemed to me the first thing to be done was to get hold of that letter. I knew the fellow who had written it, a garrulous sort of chap who'd never go into court and swear he had seen this or that on any special occasion.

"That's why Edward values the letter so much," Viola told me.

"Then we've got to get hold of it."

"But how?"

"Can't you get it off him?"

"He will carry it about with him night and day until he takes it to a lawyer."

"When will that be?"

"He says there is a private detective coming down tomorrow."

"Then we must get it before tomorrow."

"But how?"

"You say he's working late tonight?"

"He will be asleep until about eleven-forty-five. He has set the alarm. He sleeps very deeply."

"So one could slip up to the room—does he undress?"

"Oh, yes. Entirely."

"The letter would probably be in one of his pockets."

"I couldn't do it," said she. "Besides, what would be the use? He would miss it and he would know I had taken it."

"I'll get it," said I in the tone of a man who has nothing to lose. If Teddy Ross meant to take action

I was in the soup already. We came back to the house; it was eleven twenty-five when we reached the corner of the street, and found an amorous couple lurking in the shadow of the laburnum tree in the garden of The Laurels.

"We can't go in now," I said. "They'd be sure to see us."

We walked past the corner, around the square, back the other way. The couple hadn't budged. It was eleven-forty before it was safe for us to go into the house. There wasn't a light burning anywhere. I'll swear to that. Wright may have been awakened by the clashing of the gate, but he didn't see us come up the path. Viola had a latchkey, and we came in with no particular regard for sound. Teddy would be asleep; Martha was deaf.

"Which is his room?" I asked.

"He sleeps in Harry's room now. It's on the right at the top of the stairs."

I went up on stockinged feet. When I opened the door the moonlight lay like a sheet over the bed. Teddy was sleeping; he looked more furtive, more rat-like than ever, with his teeth in a glass by the bedside. His clothes were bundled untidily on a chair. I began feverishly to search through the pockets. I was still hunting when my eye fell on the clock. The alarm had been set for eleven forty-five and it wanted only a minute to that time. Teddy looked as though he was already in his last long sleep. I crossed the room hurriedly, picked up the clock. It was a new sort of mechanism, I couldn't see how to switch off the alarm. I looked around me. I'd have chucked it out of the window, but I was afraid of questions being asked in the morning. There was a hat box by the wall and I pulled off the lid and wrapped the clock in a scarf that was inside.

But I was a couple of seconds too late. As I picked up the scarf the bell began to ring. Teddy Ross woke instantly. He turned over on his back and opened his eyes. He saw me, of course. He couldn't help it. He opened his mouth. In an instant, acting on instinct, I had picked up a small pillow from a neighboring chair and crushed it over his face. I never had any thought of killing him. I simply wanted to make him be quiet. I said, "If I take this thing away will you shut up?" He didn't answer. Naturally. He couldn't. Then I took it away and he just lay there and didn't move. I couldn't speak for a minute. There are some things so bad you can't believe them. At first I thought he was dead, and then I knew that was absurd. I touched his shoulder.

"It's all right," I said. But it wasn't. Nothing's ever going to be all right for me again.

I found I had the cushion in my hand and I threw it into a chair. I didn't think of it being stained with blood. Even if I had known I couldn't have done anything. Then I saw the letter. It was on the mantelpiece, weighted down by a china ornament. I took it instinctively. If I'd seen it when I first came in I needn't have killed him. Because by now I did realize he was dead. That is to say, I knew it without exactly believing it. I couldn't believe that men die so easily. I couldn't begin to think about the consequences. All I knew was that I had to get out of the house as soon as possible. I never gave another thought to the clock.

"I've got the letter," I told Viola.

"You'd better burn it," replied she.

"I thought I'd tear it to shreds and put it in the basket."

"You don't know my husband. The first thing he'd do would be to piece it together again, and things would be worse than ever. You oughtn't to wait, Richard. He will be down any minute now."

I just prevented myself from saying that it didn't matter what we did with the letter, that he couldn't piece it together when he came down, because he would never be coming down again. I muttered something incoherent and put on my shoes.

Viola opened the front door for me. "We shall meet on Friday," she said. "As usual."

"As usual," I repeated. I didn't care what promises I made. I only wanted to get away. I never thought about neighbors snooping. I didn't notice a light in the window of the house next door. I went straight back to my own place and went to bed. It was an appalling night. I heard the clock strike every hour; at four o'clock I got up and drank a stiff peg of whisky. As I put the glass down I thought, "It's only four hours and it seems like a year already." I wondered what had happened at The Laurels, if Viola had found him, what she thought. It might look as though he had died in his sleep. Everyone knew his heart was weak. Then I remembered her saying that she was going straight to bed, she didn't want to see him any more that night, so probably nobody knew yet, no one but myself. The endless night wore on. In the morning I wouldn't go out.

I forced myself to sit at my desk and make a pretense of work. I wasn't going to ask questions, arouse suspicion. Viola didn't telephone, nobody telephoned. I sat staring at my typewriter. I didn't write a line. After lunch I went for a walk. There were some schoolboys on the same side of the road. They were talking.

"Rum old bird, Teddy," said one. "Fancy sparking out like that."

"Praise the pigs he hadn't had time to correct my impot," said another and the third chimed in, "Ill wind that blows no one any good."

"Do you suppose we shall be expected to go to the funeral?" asked the first.

"They'll probably expect us to buy him some flowers," added the second gloomily. "Rotten waste of money, if you ask me. . . . "

I walked past them unnoticed. Hope was lifting her head in my heart. If there had been any talk of foul play those boys would have heard. It would go down as death from natural causes, I should pack my bag and get out. Convention would forbid my marrying Viola for twelve months and anyway, as I've said, I didn't mean to marry her. Twelve months hence the affair would be as dead as mutton. By that time, I thought, she'd have found some other man. As for Bunty—but it was difficult to think of Bunty at such a time. In fact, all I really wanted was to be safe— safe from Viola, safe from the hangman. I might have guessed I should never be safe from either of them.

Then the news came through. There'd been police at the house. Irene Cobb was talking. Then followed the news of Viola's arrest. I was absolutely staggered. Somehow I'd never thought of this. For twenty-four hours I hung about expecting to see the police on my doorstep. But nothing happened. Viola was in jail, Teddy was in his grave. I was a free man—technically free that is. Throughout our intimacy I'd never been enslaved by Viola as I was now, when she couldn't see or speak or write to me. I knew there was one thing I had to do—I had to get her off. And I didn't want to swing for it myself. I didn't care who else swung.

It was a shock, and an ironic one, to be nominated for the jury. I thought that might be my chance, I might be able to persuade them, but that I couldn't do. I could only hold matters up for a bit, while I tried to find a substitute for the gallows. Viola told the truth all through. She had known nothing of her husband's death until a servant brought her the news next morning. She hadn't been into his room that night. Nobody believed her. She might have cleared herself by implicating me, though the odds are most people would have believed her an accessory after the fact, at least. You don't send your lover up to the room where your husband's sleeping unless you're a pretty queer sort of wife, they'd have argued. Of course, she must have known I was guilty, though she never said a word. No one else even suspected. I wonder how many people realize even now why the police arrested me for Fielding's death.

There is a saying Crook has sometimes quoted to

me, "What Arthur Crook says today the police will say tomorrow." I dare say it's true. Anyway, I'm not taking that chance. I'm writing this to exonerate Viola. They'll have to let her off now, though she won't have much of a time, I'm afraid. Still, women like that aren't easily broken down, and at least she'll have life, and life in any circumstances is worth having. Starving, crippled, nameless, derided, it's still better to be alive than mouldering in the grave. You remember Balder?

Better to live a slave, a captured man
That scatters rushes in his master's hall,
Than be a crowned king here and rule the dead.

Yes, far, far better, but it's too late to think of that now.

Looking back I can see the mistakes I made. I ought to have known it was mad to send those letters to Bunty. That was my first mistake. Of course, the early ones were typed on my own machine, but I had no intention of letting Crook or the police see them. Later, I arranged to have them stolen at the same time as I fixed up the gun in the bush outside the window. I didn't see how they'd ever trace the gun to me. I had picked it up at an auction a long time before and never used it. I had no reason to suppose they could trace it to Harry Ross either, but I hoped that a sequence of events, all of them criminal in intention, all of them involving him, would turn suspicion in his direction. The bath was the worst mistake. I never meant Fielding to die. I meant to be a bit choked myself and then call for assistance. I couldn't have foreseen that Bunty would choose that precise moment to ring me up. The needle was a trivial affair; I never expected to prove anything from that, but it was all grist to the mill, a straw to show the way the wind blew. As for the poison in the whisky, that was the most dangerous attempt of all. Poisons react differently on different people, I'd been told, but I had to take the chance. Crook isn't the only man who knows London's underside. There wasn't much trouble buying the stuff and no chance of identification, and I'd been lucky in discovering that one of the gang with whom young Ross went to the dog races was involved in the drug trade. Of course, what I hadn't allowed for, what I couldn't have allowed for, was Wright's evidence. But for that I might not be here now. But I was afraid of the truth coming out, I thought I must destroy that diary. I don't know quite what I meant to do when I went to his house that night. Some things have to be left to chance, and it seemed to me chance had played a very pretty card on my side. But as it happened that was my undoing.

I don't think there's much to add. I suppose I should say something about Bunty but she seems so far away from me now it's like another world. Anyway she'll be all right. There's Derek Markham, and if it isn't him there'll be someone else. The Buntys of this world don't go wasted to the grave.

I've always wanted to achieve fame with my books. Now I suppose I've done it. Everyone will read this last book of mine. It'll go on selling long after I've rotted under the prison flags. But at least, I'm going to spare myself the suspense, the misery, the death endured a hundred times that is the fate of men condemned by their country to die. It's an odd legal expression that—to throw yourself on your country, the country being represented by twelve little anonymous men and women in a box. I've always been prepared for this emergency. In a corner of my handkerchief there's a tiny tablet. They didn't discover it when they searched me. I've got to do it tonight. Tomorrow will be too late. I shall manage it all right. It only takes a second when the warder's back is turned. And this is instantaneous.

I can hear the sullen beat of rain against the walls. Occasionally a foot goes by. I wonder if anyone ever gives a thought to the men inside the building. Probably not. Life's a pretty tough game for most people; you've got to get what you can. With all that rain there won't be any stars, and if there were I shouldn't see them. It's queer to think I'll never see stars again. Being here is like being in a desert of life. Tomorrow everywhere else lights will shine, voices and laughter will sound, there'll be traffic in the streets and postmen will call at this house and that. There may be letters for me, but I shan't see them. For Viola there'll be liberty. I envy every beggar in the streets tonight. I've killed two men and I'd gladly have let another die. That's my record. I haven't even been a great writer. More than anything else, I think, I mind the fact that I shall have no opportunity to make any use of all I've learned that I never knew before.

EPILOGUE

Up and down the streets in every big city in the country ran the newsboys. "Suicide Attempt in Prison" they shouted, and "Accused Man's Dramatic Statement." The papers sold rapidly. Warm from the press they were passed over heads and under arms. "Sold Out," said the old man at the top of Henriques Square, the man with a wooden leg, who sat on a cane-seated chair outside the tobacconists. And to himself he added, "Pity they can't find anything better to write about."

The Ross case—Fielding's name was scarcely mentioned—was arousing universal excitement which increased as the weeks went on. Richard Arnold's confession, his abortive attempt at self-destruction, the trial, the acquittal of Viola Ross who had lain for weeks under a capital charge and had already faced the horror and odium of a public trial, all these combined to make the affair as sensational as any during the past twelve months.

The gossip writers got hold of it, gloated over it. "Dorothea" in the *Sunday Record* wrote: Saw exotic looking Mrs. Edward Ross, this week's heroine, stepping into a train for I won't say where, last night. She has, as you know, just been released on a murder charge from prison and actually had to give evidence in the charge against her former lover. Men may condemn but women everywhere will remember her as the woman who knew that love covers a multitude of sins. Greater love hath no man than this, that a man shall lay down his life for his friends. And that, sisters, is what Viola Ross was prepared to do—for love."

A more enterprising journalist raised another point. Can the confession of a man who is found to have committed suicide while of unsound mind be regarded as valid? Suppose Richard Arnold had been successful in his attempt, could his document have been accepted as evidence? Since Arnold had not been successful and in any case any reasonable jury would have found him guilty of *felo de se,* the point did not arise, but it gave a number of busybodies an admirable opportunity to write long letters to the papers expressing opinions that were, naturally, quite valueless.

Meanwhile the law held to its course. Three weeks after he had been found guilty of murder Arnold, again in the jargon of the press, paid the supreme penalty. Viola Ross disappeared. Energetic reporters traced her as far as Fenland, but after that, like the tracks of Lucy Grey in Wordsworth's immortal snow, "footsteps there were none." It was generally supposed that she had either gone abroad or that her body would subsequently be discovered in some remote place where she had gone to destroy the life for which, once, she had fought so desperately.

Actually she had concealed herself, like a needle in a bundle.of hay, in one of those anonymous private hotels with which London abounds, joining the great army of women, the flotsam and jetsam of civilization, spinsters, widows, deserted wives, all gleaning their little sparks of brightness from such contacts as their circumstances enable them to make, all resolutely and with the courage at their disposal getting what they can out of the monotonous days, whose purses are as thin as their experience of life or their hopes of the future.

The events of the past week had so changed her that she had little difficulty in concealing her identity; a sense of alien life possessed her; even her face had altered, its vivacity had gone, only a kind of fierce resolution, a chill and bitter anger, now gave personality to the once notable features.

On this particular morning she saw the newsboys racing past, saw the great black letters comprising the name of her lover, on a yellow ground. Arnold executed. And she hadn't lifted a finger to save him.

She stood for a long time at the window before at length on a long breath she threw up her head and turned away.

"So that's the end," she said aloud. "Richard is buried and the truth's buried with him. Now no one will ever know."

Here, however, she made a mistake. At that identical moment in his crow's-nest of an office, Arthur Crook was observing to Parsons, "Another case of justice done in the eye, old boy. You know, I admire that woman."

"What woman?"

"Mrs. Ross. She knows how to keep her mouth shut and that's a rare feat in her sex."

"She talked enough at the trial."

"Everything except essentials. That's a woman all over."

"What was the essential she didn't speak of?"

"A trifling matter—the actual identity of her husband's murderer."

Bill stared. His mouth fell open. "You mean—"

"Missed that, did you?" asked Crook in high spirits. "I wondered. All the same, I wonder if the police missed it, too. Most likely not, but they knew there wasn't a damn thing they could do and this chap had confessed. Anyhow, he deserved the rope. He was a muddler. He pulled off a murder and swung for it, but that was an accident. When he was on the job he mucked it up every time. Edward Ross's murder, Harry's, his own. Each time he just missed the bus. I hate these chaps who can't even kill a man when they set their minds to it."

"Then who the devil did murder Ross?"

"His wife, of course. Though, mark you, Arnold died without knowing that. Did you read the evidence? He says that the old man turned over on his back and he pressed the pillow over his face. Well?"

"Well?"

"Read the evidence at Mrs. Ross's trial. Edward Ross was found lying on his side. Dead men can't move themselves."

"You mean, she went in afterwards? . . . "

"Certainly I mean that. I expect Arnold looked a bit queer when he bolted out of the house. I should say she went up and found the old boy struggling back to consciousness. He may even have been able to talk. Anyhow—she's a quick-witted woman—she grasped the situation, she knew whatever happened he mustn't be allowed to spread his yarn, so she up and wiped Arnold's eye for him."

"And let him swing for it?"

Crook shrugged his great shoulders. "My Scotch sense approves that. As the prince in the fairy tale observed, why should two die where one will suffice? Arnold was going to die anyhow for the Fielding affair —though, mark you, Bill, she'd have let him die anyway. She was one of those single-track women, and if ever you're thinking of gettin' married, avoid 'em like a plague. They've driven many a good chap under the daisies. When she heard that Arnold had been makin' love to this girl she would have had him boiled in oil —and stood by and watched the fun. Murdering her husband was a small thing—in fact, she'd probably have thought the devil of a lot of him for it. Even having a shot was something. As I told Arnold, when you're dealing with the sex, remember vanity's the middle name of the best of 'em—and I wouldn't, for all my admiration of her—for I do like a woman to know her own mind—I wouldn't class Mrs. Ross among the best.

"Letting Arnold swing was no sort of penalty for what he'd done, and he was a bit of a cad, even according to my notions, and I don't expect much from the race, Bill. Experience has shown me the dam' idiocy of that. I bet you no one was gladder to see that fellow in the dock when the judge put on the black cap than the woman who'd thought he was worth committing murder for."

"And the police didn't think of that?"

"The police think of most things, Bill. You have to hand it to 'em for that. But what could they do? They could say, you must have gone in, because there's a discrepancy in the evidence. She'd only had to say she hadn't and they were balked. It's easy for a man in a panic to make a mistake. Perhaps Ross never did turn on his back; perhaps in the struggle he turned over again. Only, I'm damn sure he didn't. No, no, the police did what I'd have done in the circumstances —kept their mouths shut."

"And the sacred cause of truth—that sun of suns, moon of moons and star of stars, as old Chadband puts it?"

"Are you asking me?" demanded Crook, incredulously. "Run away and play, Bill. What do *I* know—or care—about justice? I'm a lawyer, ain't I? When virtue runs this world, you'll find me checking in for the dole, and I'm very comfortable as I am, thanks."

The telephone rang. Crook lifted the receiver and listened attentively. "And you're innocent, of course," Bill heard him say. "You just want me to prove it? Well, that's my job." The conversation went on.

"Funny how these virtuous folk don't realize there's a premium on the goods they handle," he observed, hanging up the receiver at last. "You expect to pay insurance on a fur coat or a diamond ring, but they expect innocence to be free gratis and for nothing. This man does. Virtue's expensive, I told him. So damned luxurious that hardly anyone even tries to afford it these days."

"Did he believe you?"

"I couldn't say that at present," returned Crook equably, but there was a gleam in his eyes that might have made his prospective client quail, "but he'll learn, Bill, trust me, he'll learn."

>>> If you've enjoyed this book and would like to discover more great vintage crime and thriller titles, as well as the most exciting crime and thriller authors writing today, visit: >>>

The Murder Room
Where Criminal Minds Meet

themurderroom.com